PRAISE FOR BUILT ON SAND

'With a psychogeographer's sensibility and a deep connection to history, Paul Scraton's *Built on Sand* offers us a tender, fresh, and moving portrait of Berlin.'
— Saskia Vogel, author of *Permission*

'Sublime... Scraton has taken the broken memories of a city, refashioning them into a novel that's skewed and wondrous.'
— Irenosen Okojie, author of *Speak Gigantular*

'Cities are made of stories, and Paul Scraton's novel-in-stories is wonderfully made of the city of Berlin.'
— Lauren Elkin, author of *Flâneuse*

'Humane and ambitious.'
— Amy Liptrot, author of *The Outrun*

'A story built from fragments, together forming a stereoscopic vision of Berlin and the lives lived in its sunken streets, masterful in its attention to topographic history.'
— Jessica J. Lee, author of *Turning: Lessons from Swimming Berlin's Lakes*

'A haunted and haunting novel about the way the past is sometimes more real than the present.'
— Owen Booth, author of *What We're Teaching Our Sons*

'Paul Scraton will show you a version of Berlin you haven't seen before... An intoxicating celebration of a place.'
— Linda Mannheim, author of *Above Sugar Hill*

ALSO AVAILABLE FROM
PAUL SCRATON AND INFLUX PRESS

Ghosts on the Shore (2017)

Built on Sand

Paul Scraton

Influx Press
London

Published by Influx Press
49 Green Lanes, London, N16 9BU
www.influxpress.com / @InfluxPress
All rights reserved.
© Paul Scraton, 2019

First edition 2019. Printed and bound in the UK by Clays Ltd., St Ives plc.

Paperback ISBN: 978-1-910312-33-9
Ebook ISBN: 978-1-910312-34-6

Editors: Dan Coxon and Gary Budden
Cover Art: Austin Burke
Design: Vince Haig

'The Haunted Land' first appeared in *The Lonely Crowd* #11

For Katrin and Lotte

I

The Mapmaker

The city was shifting. As Annika drew her maps, from the initial sketches to the moment she scanned her inked lines onto a computer, she could track the changes. And from the moment she was finished, she complained, they were already out of date. Something would have been added to the city, something taken away. A gap filled-in or a hole created. On her drawing table by the window she unrolled a work-in-progress, and stabbed her finger at the heavy paper in exasperation.

'Here. Here. And here.'

She would ask whether she should change it, whether she should attempt to keep up with the developments as best she could, but the answer was always no. Yes, the city was shifting, as uneasy on its foundations as it had ever been; but on the map it would be solid, fixed in place. Her job was to capture a moment. If Annika would always be thwarted in her attempt to show the city as it was now, she would be able to hold in her hand the city as it had been.

*

To draw her maps, Annika would start by going for a walk. It was a key part of the process, along with trips to the library to source old maps and photographs, explorations of antiquarian bookstores and market stalls, as well as the hours spent navigating the virtual city through the glow of a backlit computer screen. Sometimes she would sketch out her walk in advance, when the theme for the map was fixed and the key locations already known to her. Other times she would simply set off and see what she could find. Her walks were slow, sometimes only a kilometre per hour, as she attempted to take in and document everything she saw along the way. For some maps, a single walk was enough. For others, she headed out two, three or more times, to different corners of the city. The most walks she took for a single map was thirty-two, passing through the very heart of Berlin before skirting its edges. A GPS system in her phone tracked her as she went, recording time and distance, creating a red line on a map to show her the route she had taken. After the walk came more trips to the library, to dig into the clues she had discovered along the way. All this came together, the photographs, the maps, the notes and the sketches, as she sat down at her drawing table, the blank sheet of paper rolled out in front of her, and she began to draw.

The maps were produced at a printworks in the north of the city, housed in a red-brick factory building between the prison and the airport. Annika visited once during the process, to check on the colours and the paper, before the machines began to roll and fold, the maps piled into boxes that were delivered to her apartment, to be stored with the rest on shelves in her bedroom. These were limited edition maps, fold-out pamphlets that she sold each weekend on a stall at the art and book market down by the river. Before she left Berlin the first time, the series ran to sixteen individual maps, each telling a particular story of the city. We had them all, lined up in a row on the bookshelf by the desk. One was framed, and hung on the wall above the sofa. One remained hidden away, kept by K. at the bottom of the drawer, in the cabinet that stood by her side of the bed.

Annika called the series *A Way of Seeing*, and along with the art and book market, she also supplied maps to a small number of bookstores and galleries, held exhibitions in Berlin and beyond the city, as well as launches of each edition that increasingly gained interest from the media. The maps made Annika very little money, certainly not enough to cover the rent of her small flat, which she paid for through work for others, creating logos, flyers, business cards and other graphics for various companies. That was only for the money. If people asked her what she did, she would show them, pulling out a proof copy of her very first map (*A Way of Seeing 01: Joseph Roth*) that she kept in her leather bag for that eventuality. There was no mention of graphic design work, of websites and business cards, nor the German lessons she gave to the international staff of multinational companies and start-ups. None of that was important. Just the maps.

For that first map, Annika had charted the Berlin locations linked to the writer Joseph Roth, who lived in the city in the early 1920s and who continued to return until 1933, when the Nazi ascent to power was completed and Roth went into exile. For Annika, nothing would ever be as exciting as that moment the first set of maps arrived from the printers, and she sat in her small flat to sign and number them, before loading a box onto her bicycle for the ride across town to Karl-Marx-Allee. The launch event was held in a small cafe on the ground floor of one of the huge socialist classicist housing blocks that framed each side of the boulevard. The blocks were designed by Hermann Henselmann, who would become one of the subjects of *A Way of Seeing 11*. There were a number of maps devoted to individuals, including Rosa Luxemburg and Käthe Kollwitz, David Bowie and Bertolt Brecht. Other maps focused on wider themes, from West Berlin punk to the literature of the GDR. On just a couple of occasions, she provided a guide to a specific locale. For *A Way of Seeing 14*, Annika roamed the Tiergarten, charting the hidden corners of the park where Jehovah's Witnesses once met in secret under National Socialism, and she told the story of the East German stonemasons who were brought through the Wall to West Berlin to carry out essential repairs to the Soviet War Memorial. The map also remembered the Love Parade, and the time Christo wrapped the Reichstag. It reminded those who looked at it about the Nazi exhibition that told Berliners what it meant to be a German, and which took place in the palace that would later be home to the German president. All the layers of the Tiergarten's history went into the map, all those stories, piled atop the soil of the old royal hunting grounds.

The maps were not useful navigation tools. Annika prescribed no route for the readers to follow and these were not walking tours. If the locations were spread out across the city, the map would take liberties with distance and the liberal use of empty white space to create a series of islands, a cultural archipelago where each destination was surrounded by just a handful of streets. In the white blank spaces, Annika encouraged readers to make their own additions and add their own details. Sometimes she included street names. Sometimes she left them off. And sometimes she used the old names, as they would have been when Joseph Roth or Rosa Luxemburg stalked the streets.

Although all her maps were contained within the city limits of Berlin, Annika's longest walk took her on a train south to Dessau as she prepared for *A Way of Seeing 09*. She returned to the city on foot, attempting to follow the route taken by fourteen-year-old Moses Mendelssohn in 1743. When he made the walk, Berlin was much smaller and surrounded by a city wall. On arrival from the south, he was forced to skirt the city boundary until he reached the Rosenthal Gate, the only entrance to the city that Jews were permitted to use. It was also the only gate through which it was permitted to bring cattle into the city. Annika skirted the old city limits, following an imaginary wall before passing through an imaginary Rosenthal Gate. Once there, she was not far from her apartment and the cemetery where, forty-three years after he entered the city, the German-Jewish philosopher Mendelssohn was buried. It was there, next to Mendelssohn's burial site, that the Gestapo would, much later, turn a home for the elderly and a Jewish boys' school into a collection point and internment centre for the Jews of the neighbourhood.

From there, they were transported to Grunewald station in the west of the city and loaded onto cattle trucks, deported to the extermination camps to the east. Having removed the living, the Gestapo attempted the same with the dead. They destroyed the cemetery and desecrated the graves. It would later become a mass burial site for the victims of bombing raids near the end of the war, as three thousand more bodies were added to the three thousand, including Mendelssohn, who had long been resting there.

When Annika moved into her apartment around the corner, the school had been reopened, the cemetery cleared once more and planted with a neat lawn. Outside the gate, a memorial to those taken to the camps was installed, while inside, a few symbolic headstones had been restored, including that of Moses Mendelssohn. Otherwise the grounds were empty, save the grass and the gravel pathways. It sent, Annika would say, a gently perfect message to those who walked by and looked through the iron fence to the grounds beyond. It was a reminder, she said, of what had been lost.

Annika loved that apartment, with its two rooms, tiny galley kitchen and bathroom that had somehow been squeezed into the hall, overlooking a churchyard on a street where Franz Biberkopf met a red-bearded Jew in the early pages of *Berlin Alexanderplatz* and where, each winter, we would meet beneath her living room window to have mulled wine during the Christmas Market. Over the years that she lived there, Annika noted the changes to her neighbourhood. She watched as, one by one, the squats established in the 1990s were shut down and the buildings tidied up. She noted the long absence of a homeless man, previously a fixture by the tram stop on the corner, until she learned from a neighbour that he had died during a particularly cold winter. Above his chair someone fixed a picture of him that survived as a memorial until the road was dug up to lay new water pipes, and when the construction site was removed, his empty chair and the photograph were gone. One evening, she realised that the prostitutes, who had arrived with the fall of the Berlin Wall to work the street just down from the synagogue, had at some point moved on. She had grown so used to their presence that she had stopped noticing them when they were there, and it was only their absence that brought them back to mind.

Despite these shifts, Annika clung to the fixtures of her neighbourhood, from the churchyard and the memorials to her regular dance lessons at the old ballroom down the street, where she moved beneath the glitter ball and the cartoons on the wall depicting the characters of a long-lost Berliner *milljöh*. On her way home from the dances, feeling the cold Berlin air meeting the heat of her sweat-drenched body, she whistled an old music hall tune.

So schwindest Du hin, Du mein altes Berlin...

The song was from deep in the memory of the city, the lyrics mourning the changing nature of an older version of Berlin. It was always the same story.

As she continued to work on the series, the maps began to consume Annika's time in a way that the earlier works had not. *A Way of Seeing 15* took over her life for more than a year, as she moved from one library or archive building to the next, in an attempt to trace the history of witchcraft and the witch trials held in the area of present-day Berlin. The main period covered by the map was the sixteenth to eighteenth centuries, and the towns and villages that once surrounded Berlin, later swallowed and reimagined as new city districts and neighbourhoods. The last ever witch trial, documented on the map, took place in what would become the district of Wedding, not far from where K. and I lived in a nineteenth-century tenement block, built to house the factory workers that transformed an old village surrounded by marshes, forests and lakes into the industrial powerhouse of Berlin. As always, Annika walked the neighbourhood, and although there was nothing to be seen of the old village, she lingered on street corners, locating the likely site of the witch trial where she waited to get a sense of the place, a feeling, that she could include on her map.

For the same map she travelled through the old villages of the north and the south, to Malchow and Falkenberg, Marienfelde and Lichtenrade, seeking out medieval churches and early modern farmhouses that had not been bulldozed by the expanding city. She followed the old ways that had once linked them, searching out the places where memorials had been erected and records kept. She uncovered traditions still maintained, including *Walpurgisnacht* celebrations to greet the witches as they passed by on their way to dance on the slopes of the Brocken mountain, and she immersed herself in the stories of the Thirty Years War and the tales of marauding armies, plague and famine. Devil-worship was a logical response to such times, Annika thought, as was a rising belief in ghosts, phantoms and spectres. The fault for misfortune was laid at the doors of black magicians, and there was plenty of misfortune about. Most of all, it was laid at the door of women, who would be tried and executed in their tens of thousands.

'Imagine that number of people killed for their religion or race...' Annika said to us, as the map neared completion. And she wrote those words down, and left them hanging, along the bottom of the map. It was the map that offered the least to see on street level, but it was Annika's most beautiful creation, filled as it was with her illustrations based on woodcuts, sketches and etchings she had found during her research. She presented images of the women accused of witchcraft, because she believed it told us something important, and not just about how things were then.

She gathered together so much material that it threatened to swallow her apartment whole. When the map was finished, her boyfriend Adam encouraged her to throw most of it away. She needed, he said, to get her living space back. There's a good chance that he also meant her life. But Annika simply found some order to her collection, gradually formalising the sketches, maps, illustrations and extracts from dusty, long-forgotten library books into an exhibition of sorts. She invited people to view it via a handwritten note taped beside the doorbells and a poster on the wall. Annika loved to hear the bell ring, to invite the strangers up into her apartment and show them the result of her work.

One day the bell rang; it was her landlord. He took his time to look through Annika's DIY museum, accepting the invitation of a cup of tea. He agreed with her that this was an important part of Berlin's history, and one that had long been neglected. But the neighbours had complained about the number of visitors on the stairs, so he would have to ask her to stop.

✳

It was around that time that Annika's boyfriend, Adam, decided to leave the city. He had found a house overlooking the drained polders of the Oder River and the Polish countryside beyond. It was a chance to escape, he said, as he persuaded Annika to go with him, to give up the flat that faced the churchyard, and move to the house on the very edge of the country. She did not require much persuading, as she often expressed a desire to leave Berlin behind her. She told us the news as we sat on our balcony on the top floor of our old tenement block. From there we could look north above the rooftops of the city, to the gentle rise of an old rubbish dump transformed into parkland and the wind farms turning above the horizon. They represented the world beyond the city limits, which was why Annika liked to sit up there. Living in the city, she would say, sitting on our balcony, it was important to be able to see your way out. When she lived in Berlin she came by once a week, to sit with K., drink and smoke, and imagine the world beyond the rubbish tip.

Before they left Berlin, we went with her in our Skoda, driving east to take a look at the house Adam and Annika had bought with money they had somehow scraped together. On the way we stopped above the marshland that stretched out from the Seelow Heights towards the border, parking beneath a Soviet War Memorial that looked down on a landscape which had cost the lives of so many in the final weeks of the war. From this drained land there had long been stories of soldiers' bodies pulled from the peaty soil, preserved over the centuries from when they fell during the

Thirty Years War. Bodies continued to be found, turned over by the farmer's plough, but now they were as likely to be fallen Wehrmacht or Red Army soldiers as they were fighters from an earlier conflict. Layers of trauma, Annika said, piled on the land. As we walked back to the car, she told us she was sure the people there still believed in ghosts.

There was one map – *A Way of Seeing 13* – that Annika never sold. It was never to be found in the neat piles at the market stall by the river, or on the shelves of the bookstores and galleries that stocked her work. On her website it was marked as AUSVERKAUFT, but in truth it had never been for sale. Only two copies of the map had ever been produced. One for Annika, and one for K.

The map was subtitled *Where We Came From*, and it was another of Annika's islands, consisting of a grid of streets about six blocks across and four deep, a patch of forest with a small lake on one side and an S-Bahn station with lines leading out from it on the other. This was the only map for which Annika did not take a walk; the only map that required no visits to the library or virtual explorations online. It was created out of her head, out of her memory. She knew every square metre of this island, and she could return to it whenever she chose.

She did not need to walk the island because it was a map of the small collection of streets where she and K. had grown up, a few doors down from each other on the edge of the forest. It was here, in West Berlin, that they had met at primary school and then, in what was by now a reunified city, attended the same high school. It was here that they climbed the oak trees K.'s father told them were hundreds of years old, and explored the sand dunes created by the mass excavation of earth needed to help build the city. It was here that they swam in the lake, stripped down to their naked bodies when there was no one else around. And it was here that they ducked under fences onto railway sidings for first cigarettes and bottles of beer, climbed the walls of the empty football stadium to sit on the terraces with an inexpertly rolled joint, and disappeared into the woods for early sexual encounters. All were faithfully recorded on the map, in a code Annika knew K. would understand.

STEFAN (A). F/B. ALMOST.

Stefan made an appearance again, elsewhere on the map. A different moment and a different entry. This time marked (K). This time there was no more almost.

It was the map of a place and of a specific period in their lives, but what it did not show were the forces that were beginning to pull the two friends apart. Or perhaps it did. K. would say that *A Way of Seeing 13* told you all you needed to know about how Annika saw the world. Annika was happy on those ten streets and with that patch of forest. Annika wished she had never had to leave.

'If I had drawn the map,' K. said, finger pressed down on the railway line leading off the side of the illustration, 'it would have started, not finished, here.'

Their neighbourhood was part of Berlin, but as kids it might as well have been a village in the countryside. And while Annika was content in her village, on her island, K.

could see the possibilities of the city that lay elsewhere, further along that S-Bahn line. She understood that there was something more out there, something other than the tennis club and the lake, and the fumbling fingers and dry tongues of her classmates in the suburban edgelands. That was the moment they began to drift apart. It was only later, after Annika had followed her to the city, that they resurrected their friendship in new surroundings.

Before she followed Adam to the house that looked out across the border, Annika completed her sixteenth map. It involved walking the entire 160-kilometre route of the Berlin Wall, which she did in thirty-two painstakingly slow stages. Her problem, she said, was that unlike her other maps, where there was often nothing to see and no traces to be found, here there were simply too many reminders of history to include them all. The line of cobblestones through the city centre; the memorials to those who had died; the surviving stretches of the border fortifications, the watchtowers and repurposed border guard barracks; the straight line of young trees, planted to fill the gap that had been cut in an otherwise ancient forest. *A Way of Seeing 16* turned out to be not one map, but a bundle. Six in total, tied together with a piece of string. As the time to leave Berlin grew near, there was an urgency in Annika's work. This was the biggest of all her projects and although she could have taken it with her, we sensed her need to complete it before they loaded up the van and drove east. All in all it took fifteen months, from the first walk between the Brandenburg Gate and Ostbahnhof train station, to the evening she called K. to tell her that the last of the maps was done. Adam had already left, as the final map made its short journey from the printworks to Annika's already empty apartment. Three days later, Annika followed him.

Sixteen maps. From Joseph Roth to the Berlin Wall. From punks to witches. The maps were all different, and yet they were all linked.

'This is a city of bad news,' Annika once said, and although all cities were, in their own way, for Annika it was true of Berlin more than any other. She would deliver a list, counting them off on her fingers.

War. Division. Plague. Rape. Murder of women. Disease. Murder of Jews. Bombs. Murder of gays and of gypsies and asylum seekers. Ruins. Failed revolution. Successful revolution.

Bad news. Her maps, as a whole, told the story of the city, from its medieval origins on a malarial swamp to fifteenth-century riots, reformation and industrialisation, militarism and nationalism, National Socialism and communism, the Marshall Plan and the European Union. Later, after she returned to the city, she lived close to a patch of wasteland that had been filled with what were known as 'Tempohomes' – whitewashed shipping containers transformed into a refugee camp, subdivided into small apartments for families and individuals, television rooms and gyms, places to do the laundry or for children to play.

'Berlin is the city where theories are tested,' she said.

The outlier in the sixteen maps might have been the one of her childhood and adolescence, with its intensely personal subject matter, but it contained within it a clue as to what was going on throughout them all. Taken as a whole, Annika's maps were her attempt to make sense of a place she had never felt comfortable in, an attempt to know and control a city whose ghosts made her nervous. So she read, she walked and she drew, forcing herself to know and understand Berlin in its intimate detail, getting to know it better than those who loved it, from the street corner and the park bench to the tram stop, the graveyard and the smoky corner pub. She connected all the islands and filled in all the white blank space. The unfamiliar became familiar, part of the known world. There was, she seemed to believe by the end, nothing to be scared of in this city of bad news.

And yet, when Adam beckoned her to the wooden house on the ridge, above the dark forest and the flood polders stretching out to the river and the border with another country, she was only too happy to hear the siren call. When she handed in the keys to the apartment overlooking the churchyard, packing up her maps and her drawing table, her box files full of the city she was leaving behind, she was sure she was leaving for the final time. It had been enough. In sixteen maps over ten years, she had conquered the place that for so long had intimidated her at the other end of the S-Bahn line. It was because of her maps that she had not been defeated. It was because of her maps that she was able to hear the siren call at all.

II

An Empty Stool

The night before Otto died, Markus had been at the hospice with Konrad, the three childhood friends together again for the final time. Although Otto could no longer drink and was drifting in and out of consciousness, Markus and Konrad shared a small bottle of whisky before they said their goodbyes. Otto slipped away during the night, as Markus was sitting, still awake, on the balcony of his apartment, looking west towards the city centre in the distance and the blinking mast of the TV Tower. Otto's wife called him in the morning. She sounded tired, Markus told me later, but relieved that the journey, so difficult in its final stages, had reached its destination. In the end, she said, they had both been ready; a final goodbye and a kiss of cracked, dry lips to the sound of early birds beyond the hospice window, pre-empting the dawn. And then she walked home, eight kilometres through the early morning streets, sharing the pavement with newspaper delivery men, shift workers and a few stumbling drunks. As she approached the block where she'd lived with Otto for over forty years, she spotted one of the family of foxes who lived in the bushes close to the tram stop. The lights were on in the bakery. She could see Sophie, the daughter of one of her old colleagues, readying herself to open. Everything familiar, everything changed. Back home, she waited for the clock to tick on a little further before starting to work through the list that she had compiled only a few days before, but which she could barely remember writing. Otto's brother. Their nephew. Then Markus. He was still sitting on the balcony when she called, watching the shadow of his apartment block shorten as the sun rose ever higher in the sky. He had been waiting for the call. Waiting for the permission, granted with the sound of her voice, to abandon his post for the oblivion of his bed, the final vigil complete.

Markus, Otto and Konrad grew up in East Berlin in the 1950s and 1960s, in different corners of the city. They met at the age of sixteen when they were selected as part of a representative football team invited to play a friendship tournament against teams from Poland and the Soviet Union in Minsk. It was their first trip beyond the borders of the German Democratic Republic, and they caught the train from Lichtenberg station, gathering in the gloom of an autumn evening with their parents, nervously meeting teammates that, in most cases, they had only seen at the trials and for a single practice match. They were all dressed in their new tracksuits, with BERLIN/DDR on the back and the state emblem on the front, and had been told at a team meeting that they were to see themselves as representatives, ambassadors for Berlin, for the German Democratic Republic and for socialism. Markus could remember sitting through the meeting, a few days before they had gathered at Lichtenberg station, but he had not really been listening to the speeches. Instead, he had daydreamed about the journey across Poland, about what he would see once they reached the Soviet Union, and about the girls he was sure were waiting for him on the grand, wide pavements of Minsk.

The journey was long, travelling overnight from Berlin across the Oder River and into Poland, before crossing that country to reach another border and a change of train wheels to fit the gauge of the Soviet railways. From the station in Minsk, they were taken by coach to a huge hotel on the edge of the city, where they slept three to a room. Markus's roommates were also his midfield partners. Otto on the left. Konrad on the right. During the long journey from Berlin, the three boys had gone from wary greetings to the immediacy and intensity of friendship that only such travel together can create. By the time they arrived in Minsk, Markus said later, he knew those two boys better than all but his immediate family. By the time they repeated the journey on their way back to Berlin, he felt as if he knew them better than anyone.

When Markus looked back on the trip to the Soviet Union, football was only part of the story. He could remember that they won the first game, against a team from Poland, and then drew the second, against their hosts from Minsk, before being absolutely destroyed by a team of giants from Moscow, who seemed to belong to a different species entirely. In that final game, the job had been to limit the score and to save face against what was, until the final whistle, a relentless, un-fraternal onslaught. But in that battle, played in an echoing stadium of a hundred thousand empty seats, the bonds of friendship tightened. There was a photograph, taken by the team physio in the immediate aftermath of the final game. It showed the three friends arm in arm, hair plastered to their heads with sweat as they smiled toothy grins at the camera. Behind them was the pitch and a few blurred figures; beyond that, the low rake of the empty stands, filling the entire background with the exception of a tiny sliver of sky at the very top of the picture. A scoreboard in the corner documented their defeat in numerals, the team names spelled out in Cyrillic on either side. 0–4.

'It was four–nil at half-time,' Markus said, when he showed me the photograph. 'A scoreless second half was our victory.'

In truth, though, Minsk meant much more than three hard-fought football matches. It was the summer of 1968. In Prague, Dubček was in the Castle. There were demonstrations in Paris and London, Mexico City and on the streets of West Berlin. In Minsk, the three young men smuggled beers into a chaperoned youth club disco, before attempting to smuggle three young women back into the hotel with a shining red star above the entrance. In their own way, Markus said later, they had been attempting a version of the East German-Soviet friendship, cemented a month before tanks from both countries rolled out across the cobblestones of Prague to end the experiment in socialism with a human face. The boys did not think of Prague. They thought about the girls and players from the other teams, the bottles of vodka and toasts voiced beyond the earshot of coaches and those taciturn men in ill-fitting suits who had joined them on the platform at Lichtenberg and barely spoke a word. One night, the team had to carry the goalkeeper to his bed. The next night it was

Otto. They swapped addresses with their new friends, made promises to write.

'Come and visit us,' the boys said, to the girls whose names were lost to time, memory, and, scribbled on a ripped-open cigarette packet, down the side of a sleeper compartment bunk. Come to Berlin. It could be so easy. The girls couldn't come to the train station to wave them off, although Konrad especially liked to imagine that scene. Steam and dust and revolutionary songs on the platform, tears in the corner of perfectly made-up eyes and a final swig of vodka to stave off, for a moment longer, the impending feeling of loss. Markus, Konrad and Otto slept all the way back to Berlin.

Their friendship survived the journey and the return to normal life. In the GDR, a new decade brought subtle shifts, a new leader and new rules and the talk of no taboos, but it was not to last. As things shifted once more, the three friends moved in different directions towards their future roles in the workers' and peasants' republic they called home. Otto became a teacher, of maths and science, a role he would continue in both before and after the fall of the Berlin Wall. Konrad's dream was to study art, and he was placed on an apprenticeship scheme as a poster designer for a state-owned publishing company. Not long after he completed his training he refused to join his colleagues in a public parade. Later, he could not even remember what it was they were supposed to be parading in support of. It hadn't really mattered at the time. All that was important was that they turned up. Konrad timed a toilet visit long enough to miss the call across the open-plan studio and the dutiful shuffle of men and women to the door. It pained his supervisor, Konrad could tell, to have to let him go. But he did. After leaving, he found another job as a lowly assistant in a photo lab, developing wedding pictures and holiday snaps. He continued to paint, showing his dark, brooding canvases at unofficial and unapproved exhibitions, held in private apartments in the courtyards of East Berlin's crumbling tenement blocks, or the back rooms of sympathetic pubs.

'When Bismarck banned the Social Democrats,' he said, much later, 'they held political meetings under the cover of card games in the backs of pubs. We used the same spaces to show our paintings, to read our stories and to sing our songs.'

When the Wall came down, Konrad found minor fame for a while as a genuine oppositional artist, one who had never wavered or made the compromises with the regime that might have made his life a little easier. For a few years in the 1990s he even made a little money, but soon it was back to the back-street art galleries and squatted exhibition spaces, the occasional sale providing a timely boost to his small state pension. One part of Konrad's story that often puzzled outside observers was how he had managed, throughout those years in the dissident scene, to be pretty much left alone by the GDR authorities. Cynics suggested there must be something secret in his past, a skeleton called the Stasi. And there was something in this, although Konrad had never informed, never worked for the Ministry for State Security, and when the files were opened it was clear to all that his record was as clean as the blank canvases in the corner of his studio.

The truth was that, although Konrad had never asked for it and had never offered anything in exchange, in Markus, his old midfield partner, he had protection. While his friends were training to become teachers or poster designers, Markus was attending the elite high school in Berlin, before studies in Moscow and a return to the GDR for a role at the Ministry. There he was able to use his growing influence to protect his friend, even if it came at the cost of a friendship that would only partially be restored once the Wall came down. That Markus was ex-Stasi was common, if unspoken knowledge, in the pub where we all drank. It was there, not long after I first met the three men, that I asked him what it was he had done before retirement.

'I was a civil servant,' he replied. 'Government work.'

He went on to tell me that after the changes, there was no role for people like him. For his skills. He compared himself to the factory workers of the rationalised state industries, or the collective farmers no longer needed to work the reprivatised land. It was all, Markus said, from the highest corner of the Ministry to the humblest worker picking asparagus in the fields, part of the capitalist obsession with efficiency. Not that Markus saw much efficiency in the new world around him, as they moved, he said, from paying people something for doing very little, to paying people something for doing nothing. Meanwhile, those now paid something for doing nothing had lost their sense of self-worth and purpose. He supposed that for himself, he didn't really mind. He had been given early retirement on a full pension, as long as he went quietly. Even the opening of the files had little impact on him. After all, everyone had known what he did, what he had done. It was the others who had the difficulties; those who had to explain their actions, long hidden away in those dusty archives, to their friends and family once the truth came out.

The pub where we met was owned by a retired West Berlin policeman. There, Otto, Konrad and Markus had rekindled their friendship in retirement, meeting every week, except in the summer when Markus was at his cabin in the countryside. We would often see them at the end of the bar, and even on the nights they did not show up, their three stools would stand there, empty and safe and waiting for them. In the beginning, we lived around the corner and went to the pub to meet our old friend Boris, who lived in the apartment above. Later, we had to travel a bit further, and Boris was long gone, but it remained our local, remained the place where I would meet K. after work, once my tours were complete and she had finished another day at the university.

Of the three older men at the bar, K. liked Otto and Konrad, but she found it hard to warm to Markus. It was hard, she said, to get over his past. And yet it was K. whom Markus called after Otto died, finding her number on the university's website so that he could tell us the news and invite us to the funeral. Otto would have liked us both to be there, he said, and Boris too, so we scribbled a note in our diaries and left a message on our old friend's answer machine when he did not pick up, and tried to think about what we had in our wardrobe that was suitable to wear.

The day of the funeral was bright. We caught the tram from outside our apartment building to the cemetery gates, next door to a huge sports complex where the elite athletes of

29

the GDR once trained. Otto had lived around the corner. Markus, a few tram stops to the north. He was already in the chapel when we arrived, as were most of the mourners. Otto's wife sat next to Konrad, clasping his hand. Markus sat alone, across the aisle. Otto had been cremated; his ashes were in an urn at the front of the chapel, next to a photograph and bunches of flowers, placed on the floor. There were no eulogies, just music. Joni Mitchell. Fairport Convention. Bob Dylan. Once the music stopped a member of the chapel staff moved forward, solemnly lifting the urn from the ground before announcing, in a gentle but powerful voice, that we should follow Otto on his final journey. It took us down a gravel path between tall poplar trees, blowing in the breeze, before crossing a patch of grass to where a neat hole had been dug in the sandy soil.

Otto's wife approached the grave first, followed by other family members, friends and ex-colleagues. There were many of Otto's former students there to say farewell to their old teacher. K. and I hung back, waiting to go forward together. When the time came, K. knelt down on the grass and whispered something. I placed my hand on her shoulder and then, when she stood, leaned forward myself to drop a handful of soil into the hole. Moving away, we stood in the sun-dappled shade of the tall trees and watched the final goodbyes.

The last to approach were Markus and Konrad, arms around each other, as they had been on the edge of a football pitch in Minsk all those years before. And then it was over, and we were walking slowly away, unsure of whether to talk and what we could say, our feet crunching on the gravel as the wind blew the trees and we could hear the scrape of skates on the ice in the hall beyond the red-brick cemetery walls. The mourners for the next funeral were gathering in the car park, in black ties and dark dresses, and beyond, at the gates, a solitary figure who raised his arm as he saw me approach and then stepped out of sight. I found him a little way down the pavement, behind the cemetery walls, smoking a cigarette.

'You got my message.'

Boris nodded and exhaled smoke through his nose.

'I should have come in,' he said. 'But I couldn't face it.'

He looked tired. His hair was greying, at the sides and in his three-day beard. When we saw more of each other I barely noticed his appearance. In my mind he was always the Boris I had met when we were teenagers, or the young man who had welcomed me to Berlin all those years ago.

'I was here earlier. I saw you arriving. I should have come in but… ah, it was too much like Sweden. Fuck it.'

He flicked the cigarette, half smoked, onto the road.

Sweden.

With one word we were back in a small churchyard on the edge of a village, surrounded by the gently rolling countryside of Skåne. We were there to bury our flatmate and our friend. I lived with Tomas for eighteen months, shared an apartment with him and Boris for a year and a half until, from one day to the next, he was gone, and those he left behind were travelling north in a battered old Skoda to catch a ferry from Rostock, before driving inland until we reached his childhood home. I don't remember much about those two days. Not how his parents greeted us or what we did on either side of the funeral. I could remember the walk to the church with Boris and K. Boris stayed near the back, and when it came for Tomas's coffin to be lifted by his old school friends and carried outside, Boris had disappeared. It was a very different scene in Sweden to Otto's funeral in Berlin. There, the mourners were younger. The grief was tinged with the anger of someone who had gone too early, in another country, far from home. There was no traffic or other sounds of the city to compete with the pastor as he spoke over the grave, just birds and a river in the distance. And yet I understood what Boris meant. Some things were all too familiar. The blue sky, criss-crossed with vapour trails. The rustle of leaves in the wind. The feeling of senses heightened, of little details and moments that would be long remembered, like the mud clinging to the bottom of recently polished shoes, or the watering cans, hanging in neat rows above the compost heap piled high with grass cuttings and slowly decomposing flowers. The lines of headstones, the names and dates, and the stories and the worlds they contained within them.

I asked Boris if he was coming to the pub, but he shook his head. He was going to wait, until we had all left. Then he would go and say his goodbyes. I wanted to reach out to him, to take him in my arms, but I held back. Instead, I patted him gently on the shoulder as he nodded a farewell. As I walked away, I tried to work it out when it was we had stopped hugging.

Franz had opened the back room of his pub for the wake, a space normally reserved for monthly quiz nights and New Year's Eve parties. Daylight shone in through cloudy windows, creating angled columns of light, within which tiny specks of dust danced. Franz had laid out a buffet along the back wall, plates loaded with halved bread rolls topped with salami or cheese, beer glasses filled with carrot and celery sticks, meatballs and sausages, boiled eggs topped with fake caviar, and flasks of coffee and hot water for tea. When Franz retired from the Berlin police force in the 1990s and took over the pub, he inherited both the monthly quiz and the pub's decor of nicotine-stained walls surrounding dark wooden panels, mismatched furniture and a collection of regulars, including Konrad, Markus and Otto. The landlord never seemed all that keen on making changes and never attempted to put his own stamp on the place. It was as if he was simply a caretaker or custodian, the pub belonging not so much to him, but to all those he served.

The funeral party drifted in, moving through to the back room to load their paper plates before returning to the front bar, where Markus and Konrad had pulled up their usual stools. K. put her bag down at the table by the door, our regular spot. Everything was in place, but everything was different. The daylight and the smell of cleaning fluid. The burn of schnapps and the gassy beer, resting uncomfortably on an empty stomach. Without speaking to K., I knew that neither of us wanted to be there. But what else were we to do? From the moment Markus had called her at the university, the day had been blocked off.

Otto. Funeral. Noon.

A scribbled note in the diary. On the calendar in the kitchen. The rest of the day, blank.

I stepped out for a breath of fresh air. The sun was still warming the air. It wouldn't be long before Markus headed out to his cabin in the countryside, close to a lake, where he spent much of the summer. Through the door I could see Konrad and Markus sitting at the bar. It was Otto who had held them together, keeping Konrad company during the summer while Markus was at the lake, or sitting there with Markus when Konrad was absent, deep in the middle of a painting. I had rarely seen the two of them alone, without Otto. He had connected them, linking them over time, through all the years that had passed, to those boys that crossed the Polish plains together. The day of the funeral would be the last time I ever saw the two of them together. From then on, until the day Franz closed the pub for good, I only ever saw Markus sitting there alone. I would ask him how Konrad was doing, and he would tell me he was fine, that he was still around, still painting, but whether Markus actually knew this, or if it was just a guess, I wasn't able to tell.

As the afternoon turned into the evening, other drinkers diluted the mourners in the pub. Franz cleared away the buffet and turned on the music. When his late shift arrived, he came over to our table with a bottle of schnapps and some glasses. It seemed right, he said, on this day of all days, to share a drink together.

We clinked glasses.

For want of something to say, I commented that Otto had always liked it there.

Franz rolled the shot glass around in his big hand.

'Everyone needs a place where they feel they belong,' he said.

The problem was the city. Franz had always thought it, even when his particular city was only half the size that it was now. People felt lost in the millions. It was why there were allotment gardens, those colonies that seemed to fill every available space with lawns and vegetable patches, barbecues and swing sets, a little patch of land. When the cities grew, he continued, they were supposed to give the confused and frightened country people who moved to the tenements and worked in the factories something to remind them of where they had come from, and what they had left behind. A connection to the land within the anonymous city. A link to the old life. As he got older, Franz said, he was sure that everyone needed these things. Everyone, he said again, needed a place where they felt they belonged.

He poured another round of drinks.

A few years before, he continued, he had been in a pub in the north of the city. From the outside it looked normal, just like his. A front room where the drinkers congregated. A back room, mainly unused. The difference with this pub was that, down in the basement, where normally the people who lived in the apartments above would store their bikes and the clothes they never wore but didn't want to throw out, there was instead a bowling alley. To reach it you had to leave the pub, entering the stairwell past the neat line-up of post boxes and messages from the caretaker before taking a narrow staircase down, beneath the building, until you reached a genuine, American-style, ten-pin bowling lane, complete with a snug, a sitting area and a beer tap. It had once been the coal bunker, from back before central heating, when all the apartments would have been warmed by a porcelain stove in the corner of the room. Now it was the pub's secret attraction.

Franz stretched back in his seat.

He had asked the pub's landlord how it came to be. The man had been running the pub since the 1960s, and before that it had been his father's. Throughout the years of the GDR it remained in the family's hands. At some point in the early eighties, the East German authorities took over a building down the street and turned it into accommodation for visiting construction workers, who were brought in for the ambitious engineering projects that were supposed to show the world the technological, social and economic achievements of German socialism. A group of Swedish construction workers lived there for a time, as they built a new sports and leisure centre, including swimming pools and saunas, tennis courts and, in a surprising nod to the fashions of the West, ten-pin bowling lanes.

The Swedish builders worked long hours, and they were a long way from home and their families. So when they were done each evening, they tended to spend some time in the pub. The landlord had learned some English in school, so they found they could communicate quite well with each other and they became friendly, as the pub became their true home from home in the city. When the landlord discovered what they were working on, he made them an offer. If they could build him a secret bowling alley in the basement, they could drink for free for the rest of the time they were in Berlin, and any time they returned in the future. And so they did. Over the next couple of months they slowly smuggled, piece by piece, all the requisite parts to build a fully-functioning, automated ten-pin bowling lane down in the coal bunker. They finished it two weeks before they were due to travel north to the Baltic and the ferry back to Sweden. And throughout that time, during the period it took them to build the lane and the few weeks after, they never paid for a beer again.

Franz had asked the landlord if any of them had ever returned, to claim another round of free drinks or to see their bowling alley, especially later, after the Wall came down. But they never did.

'They didn't need to,' Franz said, with a shrug. 'Sometimes people just need a place for a certain period of time. Then it is time to move on.'

He held out the bottle once more but K. put her hand over the glass. It was time to go home. As we pulled on our jackets and settled the tab, I looked over to the row of stools at the corner of the bar. Markus was still there, staring into the depths of his glass. Konrad's jacket hung over his. In between them was what we still thought of as Otto's stool. A week or so later, when I returned to the pub for the first time after the funeral, to meet K. for a few drinks after work, all the stools were occupied. I didn't recognise a single person.

III

Early Works

I first met Boris in Croatia, on a narrow strip of sand that separated our apartment complex from the sea, with a view out beyond the next island to the low hills of the mainland, seemingly in a permanent haze. There had been a war here, my dad said, one that I had seen on the nightly news back home. It did not seem to have touched the island. Still, my father joked that if it hadn't been for the war we would never have been able to afford the holiday. The apartment complex was quiet, populated mainly with Germans and Croatians who had left the country when it was still part of Yugoslavia, and who were returning now to visit.

I was fifteen when we went to Croatia. I remember the flags and the shiny new uniforms at the airport, the posters by the side of the road that I could not read. The warmth of the air as we stood at dusk on the deck of the ferry, waiting to set sail for the island that the war had not touched. Boris was also on holiday. When we met on the beach he told me, in halting English, that he was from Ljubljana. It was another country now, he said, but his mother was from the island and his grandparents were still there. He was seventeen and making plans to leave. Germany, where he had an uncle, was his preferred destination. Or perhaps England. Or Ireland. He only knew that he was not going to stay in Slovenia, the homeland of his father, and he couldn't imagine living under the chequered flag of Croatia, where his mother's people came from.

'We were all from the same place,' he said to me, much later. 'And then we weren't.'

After we met on the beach, we spent much of the week together, shooting hoops on the basketball court at the back of the apartment block or wandering the coastal path with a sweating six-pack of beer in Boris's rucksack and a packet of Marlboro tucked under the sleeve of his shirt. One afternoon we took his grandfather's boat out from the main beach and guided it around the headland, to a world of hidden coves and beaches only accessible from the water.

'During the war,' Boris said, 'my grandparents could hear the guns on the mainland. My grandmother said her only wish was to lift the anchor for the whole island and sail away, out to sea. Now, she has a flag on the kitchen wall. She used to have a picture of Tito.'

One evening, Boris came to our apartment and joined us for dinner. My father attempted to make small talk while my mother sat silently on the other side of the balcony table. If he so much as looked at my younger sister, she blushed. Out at sea, I spotted the ferry making its way down the coast from Rijeka to Dubrovnik. A solo kayaker striking out from the shore in the direction of Italy. Down there, among the trees, was the stone house of Boris's grandparents, with its swimming pool and chicken run.

My father was talking about the war.

Sarajevo. Gorazde. Srebrenica. Tudjman. Mladic. Milosevic.

A list of names from the evening news.

'It must have been terrible,' my father said.

'That this could have happened in Europe,' my mother added, the first words she had spoken all evening.

Boris smiled politely and curled another forkful of spaghetti.

He told them of his plans to travel and his wish to study in Germany.

My father nodded and said yes, he had read there were many refugees from the former Yugoslavia in Germany, as if that settled matters.

'I won't be a refugee,' Boris replied, his voice soft but insistent. Silence followed. Not long after that we sneaked off with a bottle of red wine, down to the beach.

We did not speak about wars or nations; instead, we talked about music and films, our shared tastes and potential discoveries to be explored further when we got to our respective homes. We toasted our friendship with red wine, feet half-buried in the rough sand.

Later, after Boris had left Ljubljana for France, then Sweden, and finally to film school in Stuttgart, we kept in touch. First it was letters, terse and to the point, before the shift to emails. A couple of times, during university and just after, we met up. He came to visit me at my parents' during a summer vacation, and I went twice to Stuttgart, sleeping on the floor of his bedroom in the shared flat, or in the bed if he was staying at his girlfriend's apartment. She was a fellow film student and the one that took him, after graduation, to Berlin. They were to get a flat in what she said was the only city in Germany that mattered. They were to make a film together. They planned trips. To the coast and north, through Poland, to Kaliningrad and the Baltic States. To Los Angeles, to see if it was as terrible as they imagined. And to the island, where Boris would take her out in her grandfather's boat to the same coves he had shown me a few years before.

They made it to Berlin. They rented the apartment. And then, she left. Boris never told me why. I got the feeling that it was simply a case of the excitement dissipating once shopping, cleaning and the monthly struggle to pay the bills began to take over dreams of films and continent-crossing adventures. It was then that Boris moved Tomas into the spare room, a friend of a friend, and he began to work in earnest on an idea he had been thinking about from the moment he caught that first bus from Ljubljana to Trieste and on to the south of France. He told me about it in an email, hurriedly typed at an internet cafe in Marseille.

It's about the betrayal of something beautiful, he wrote. *About childhood, destruction and what is left. About how we have all, even those who stayed, been scattered to the wind.*

In Berlin, he started work on the script. Each night, after working shifts in an Irish pub under the railway tracks, he sat at his desk for a few more hours before falling asleep as the birds greeted the morning. Back then, he did not need much sleep. Just four or five hours and then he was awake, the afternoon his own until it was time to return to the pub for the next shift.

Tomas was a Swedish student at the Humboldt University, working towards a master's degree in philosophy. They were friendly if not necessarily close, thanks to the very different hours they kept, but still they would meet each day in the kitchen, to make small talk about their days or to discuss bits and pieces about the flat. One evening, as Boris prepared to go to work, they talked about money and the bills that were piling up, and made the decision to rent out the living room as a third bedroom. Boris knew someone who had long been thinking of going to Berlin, and this might be the push that was needed. On his way to work he called and left a message on my answerphone. The next day I called him back. The day after, I booked the tickets.

I met Boris on a beach, but it was always the first snow of the year that made me think of him. The first flakes, floating down onto the balcony outside our living room window. The sound of snow underfoot as I moved through an otherwise muffled city. The strange brightness of Berlin after dark, as the snow reflected the puddles of light cast by the street lamps. It took me back to those first days, landing at a frozen Schönefeld Airport to wait on the platform of what felt like a long-abandoned railway station. It was all an exercise in time travel, from the poky terminal building to the parade of kiosks beneath the platforms, the angular glass of the control room and the dusting of frost on the shattered rocks between the tracks.

Boris waited for me at Alexanderplatz, at the base of the TV Tower. When he saw me emerge from the station he hurried over to greet me with a hug, and to take one of my bags onto his shoulder. We walked north together, through the half-light of a January afternoon. The shopfronts were mostly gloomy, darkened spaces with nothing to sell. The exceptions came from a neon-lit fish tank in the window of an Indian restaurant, and the flashing invitations of a SEX KINO, three doors down. Fraying election posters hung from lamp posts, offering an alphabet spaghetti of acronyms. SPD and CDU. MLPD and the PDS. On top of a theatre, a huge sign reminded us that although the Wall might have fallen more than a decade before, this was still the OST.

Time travel, again.

The apartment was at the front of a building, a few blocks north of the theatre, on a street that had so far missed most of the redevelopment money that had flowed through the district over the previous decade. These had once been working-class tenement blocks, built around a series of courtyards, designed in the nineteenth century to bring a certain social mix to the neighbourhood. It hadn't worked. Money, and the desire to squeeze as much out of these buildings as possible, meant that the dreamed-of social mix, with white collar workers at the front of the houses and their blue collar brethren at the back, remained the lost fantasy of the city planners. Most families were crammed into single-room apartments, heated with coal ovens and with shared toilets in the stairwells. A hundred years before I moved there, the average resident of what became my neighbourhood had less living space than the inmates, a few kilometres away, behind the high walls of Tegel Prison.

It was not so bad for us. Our flat had a bedroom and a bathroom to the back, overlooking the courtyard, and two bedrooms and the kitchen at the front, with a view of the street. We did have central heating, although unlike many of our neighbours, the renovation money had run out early. The houses either side of ours had new paint jobs and double glazing, with balconies bolted onto the front and elevators onto the back, whereas ours was a crumbling mess. Wooden supports held up the few balconies that had survived the Second World War and the neglect of the long years of communism, but they were at the point of giving up. Window frames peeled, allowing draughts to sneak in, however heavy the curtains, while a whole section of the facade was covered in green mesh netting to stop pieces of plasterwork falling onto the heads of unsuspecting passers-by. The huge front door refused to lock, and the outer walls bore the scars of street battles more than half a century before. Boris would try to tell me that he could distinguish which bullet holes or shrapnel marks were created by the desperate German defenders of the city, and which were the handiwork of the Red Army as the Soviets took the capital street by street. Tomas would tell him not to be ridiculous, but Boris was insistent. It was important, he said, to know who had done what. Tomas laughed. He agreed with Boris, without question. But only if it was possible to really tell. It didn't help anyone if he was making it up.

On leaving or returning to the flat, I would often stop outside the front door, to look at the scars of a long-ago war. It seemed possible, in those moments, to imagine the sounds of troops as they marched in step down the street, in line and orderly, ready to fight as the battle approached. And then later, the chaotic more frantic later, as teenagers in ill-fitting uniforms attempted to lift heavy anti-tank guns onto shaking shoulders while the Red Army approached relentlessly, and the bullets flew and the shells exploded and the holes were created that I would later run my fingers over as I stopped outside the front door on my way to the supermarket to buy bread and a bottle of orange juice.

Our apartment was on the first floor, which meant the back bedroom, where Boris slept, got very little sunshine for most of the year, whereas those to the front did. The kitchen was slim, with a small table at the window and a mishmash of furniture surrounding the sink and the cooker that had been there since Boris moved in. Tomas's room was bare, with a futon bed beneath the window and a desk facing the wall. Books stood in stacks around the edge, as if waiting patiently for shelves to arrive and assemble themselves. Boris's room was the largest, having moved himself into the old living room, where he still had the television and couch at one end, by the door, beside the row of bookshelves that ran along the wall. My room was the smallest, long and narrow, barely wider than the window at the far end, facing the door. There was a single bed and a small table Boris had found for me at the flea market. In the eighteen months I lived there, I wouldn't add much.

That first evening, it snowed. Boris and I went down onto the street, which was where Tomas found us on his way home as we threw snowballs at each other from behind parked cars. That evening Tomas cooked, which became a feature of the time we lived together. Boris called them our 'family meals', which he ate before his shift at the pub, either in the tiny kitchen or in his room, beneath a huge schoolroom map of the *Socijalistička Federativna Republika Jugoslavija* that hung above the sofa. That first night we sat in the kitchen and watched as the snow continued to fall. When I woke the next day for my first morning in the city, Berlin was covered, silenced, slowed and serene.

*

In our kitchen, Boris hung a poster from one of his favourite films. If I close my eyes and try to remember the long evenings and nights of conversation we had there, I can see those black-and-white images as if the poster was right in front of me: the boys getting their military haircuts; the couple embracing; boys holding their guns; a naked woman. Boris sat me down to watch *Rani radovi* once, providing a running commentary as the story progressed. He made me wait through the credits, because although the film was written by Želimir Žilnik and Branko Vučićević, it also featured *additional dialogue by Karl Marx and Friedrich Engels*, and this amused him, as if they had been called from beyond the grave to contribute to this classic of Yugoslav Black Wave cinema. In a way, they had.

It was from this film that Boris took the name for his own screenplay, using the English title *Early Works*. He was also inspired by the themes, by its critique of the socialist system. For Boris, as he liked to explain to anyone who asked him about his film, the collapse of socialism in Europe, and in particular in Yugoslavia, was not the result of a flaw in the original idea, but a natural consequence of the betrayal of socialism that the system represented. This was the story he planned to tell, travelling backwards and forwards in time and geography, between Slovenia and Croatia, Bosnia and the landscapes of the former German Democratic Republic. It was a documentary, of sorts. It was a fiction, also. It combined archive footage with his own, as he moved through socialist-era housing estates, past heroic memorials and extravagant new shopping malls, holes in the ground caused by fancy housing developments, and those caused by mortar shells.

In the beginning, I took shifts at the Irish pub to pay my share of the rent. This suited Boris, because I could take some shifts from him and he could devote more time to his film. He sat in his room for hours, looking over the footage he had collected, trying to work out how he was going to pull it all together, scribbling notes beneath the huge map of a country that no longer existed and yet continued to flash before his eyes. I would knock on his door after work with a couple of beers, so I could sit with him for a while as he fretted over his work and the problems it continued to pose. Throughout that time, Boris remained convinced he would find a way to tell the story he wanted to tell, and he was sure that it would be perfect.

On other nights I could tell Boris did not want to be disturbed, and so I would sit with Tomas in the kitchen, or arrange to meet him in a bar or at a party. Later, when I spoke to others about Tomas, he was always remembered for being serious and intense, and yet it would not be for his action and activism that I remembered him. Instead, I recalled weekday morning boat trips on the Spree, a tourist activity that Tomas inexplicably loved; his joy at watching Liverpool Football Club, coming to the Irish pub to continue an obsession that had begun as a young boy in Sweden in the 1980s; the meals he would plan and produce, the pages of his cookbook splattered and crumpled. Only after all that would I think about his politics, even if it was politics that had brought him to Berlin in the first place.

'If you want to make a change,' he once said, 'you have to be in a place that matters.'

To Tomas, Berlin mattered. You only had to look at the history books.

In the summer, we would go to the beer garden at the top of the hill. It was there that he introduced me to a history postgraduate he knew from university. A few weeks later, I would meet K. again at a party. It felt, as with so much of my life at that time, like the start of things.

Every so often, Boris would come into my bedroom or knock on Tomas's door and announce it was time for a trip. It was time to get off the island for a while, he would say, and so we climbed into his Skoda to leave Berlin behind us, if only for a few hours. Sometimes K. came with us. Sometimes it was just the three of us. And sometimes it was only Boris and me. In the summer, we went in search of lakes and shady trails through the woods. In the winter, we explored abandoned army bases and off-season spa resorts. Boris rarely took his camera with him on these journeys, but he was always scouting for locations. We discovered hunting lodges used by both high-ranking Nazi officials and the party functionaries of the GDR. We ate wild boar in rural pubs and gave skinheads a wide berth in otherwise empty market squares. On those trips where all four of us went along, I sat in the back with K., my head resting on her shoulder as we listened to Boris and Tomas play out their favourite argument. It was about art and politics, and what was important.

Art, Tomas proclaimed, was just like football. It was entertainment. It could be good entertainment, without question, but that was all it could ever be. No real change would come, he would continue, through a pen or a paintbrush, from the keys of a piano or through a camera lens. Boris disagreed, and I would drift off on the back seat to the sound of their discussion, that continued all the way back to Berlin and up the stairs to the kitchen, where they would argue it out beneath the black-and-white pictures of the boys getting their haircuts and holding their guns.

After Tomas died, it was clear almost immediately that neither Boris or I would stay on in the flat. I left first, jumping on the life raft that K. offered me, moving into her small apartment a few streets away, within earshot of tolling church bells that competed on a Sunday morning with the flea market traders in the square. In a neighbourhood pub, Boris found an advert for the apartment above. It was small, but more importantly, it contained no memories. In those first months and years, we were happy to leave them behind.

We continued our trips out of the city, with Boris parking his car outside K.'s apartment and leaning on the horn until one or both of us looked out of the bedroom window. It was just the two of us on those trips by then, the unspoken agreement between K. and I that this was my chance to spend time with Boris alone. And then the trips to the countryside also stopped. The Skoda reached the end of the road and it took Boris a while to save up for a replacement. By the time he had, the tradition was broken. It had been different anyway. We should have expected it, but it still came as a surprise.

As we all tried and failed to come to terms with our loss, Boris plunged deeper into *Early Works*. He was not filming any more, just watching. In the apartment above the pub he hung his *Rani radovi* picture above the desk by the window, and attempted to write the voice-over that would accompany the mix of archive and new footage he was still shaping into some kind of order. He researched music and tried to find recordings of the songs of his childhood. Five nights a week he was still working in the Irish pub. I had moved on by then, but we would meet in the bar below his flat at least once a week. He liked going down there, chatting with the landlord or the regulars at the bar. Talking to strangers. Of the locals, he liked Otto the best, and he enjoyed talking to the old teacher and hearing his stories from the school. He was less sure of Otto's friends. Konrad's weary cynicism was tiresome, and as for Markus, the retired secret policeman, for Boris there was no getting over his past. There had been too many like him in Yugoslavia, he said. They were the ones that ruined it.

And then: the drift. Boris needed more money to finish the film properly. He had reached a dead end. When his boss at the Irish pub opened a restaurant and offered him the manager's position, he took it. With regular hours and better pay, it was a chance to save up, to build the lump sum he needed to get the film done. A few months after he started at the restaurant he moved again, to a cheaper apartment close to Ernst-Thälmann-Park, where more money could be saved.

We did not see him much after that. Once a month, in the beginning, and then a couple of times a year. When we did see him, Boris no longer spoke of the film and we eventually stopped asking. Every so often I thought of him and I would realise how much I missed him. When I eventually saw him

I got the sense he felt the same, but neither of us made any real effort to turn things around, to stop the drift. I missed our talks and our nights out and I missed our trips to the lake and through the forest. But now I was doing it all with K., as although I still didn't drive, she did, and we had bought a battered Skoda of our own.

On a February day after Otto died, I was walking close to our old apartment as the first real snow of the winter began to fall. I was outside the theatre, where the neon letters no longer placed us in the OST and the street was no longer as dark as I remembered. As the snow fell, I walked north, making tracks along the pavement as I followed the same route Boris had led me as we walked from Alexanderplatz on that first afternoon in Berlin.

Our old building was still crumbling, fifteen years after I'd first set eyes on it. It was completely covered in green netting now, and the windows and doors were boarded up. A huge sign covered three of the five floors above ground level:

306 HÖFE
URBAN CITY LIVING
EIGENTUMSWOHNUNGEN
FOR SALE
THREEZEROSIXHOEFE.COM

Beneath this beatnik Denglish real-estate poem was an artist's impression of what we would soon be able to find inside. A large wooden dining table and a flat-screen television. A slim white couple, who appeared to have no other belongings beyond an empty fruit bowl and some lifestyle magazines scattered on a glass coffee table. Through the window, an impossible view of the TV Tower. Urban City Living, imagined.

The front door was boarded up, but there were still names listed alongside the row of doorbells. PRÄMANN. BOWN. PATURI. DEAN/ORRINGER. I looked to where our names had once been printed in block capitals. I pressed a few buttons. There was no sound, no response. The network was interrupted.

I leaned against the door and looked down the street, watching the snow fall heavier than it had on that first afternoon. I could see Boris, crouched down behind the cars. I could see Tomas too, on another day, stepping out onto the pavement in the sunshine. And I saw myself, still unsure of this city and my place in it, still discovering the stories and the ghosts around every corner, stories that I would later tell others, who were newer to Berlin than I would ever be again. As I tried to read the city back then, I often wondered if I would be there enough to write stories of my own, above the cobblestones and beneath the weak light cast by streetlamps whose bulbs had not been changed since before the fall of the Wall. I wondered back then if I would ever have ghosts of my own in that city, right up until the moment when I realised I did.

That February morning, I pulled out my phone. On the poster above me the sun was shining into the open-plan apartment of the computer-generated couple, but in reality, it was cold and my fingers were numb as I swiped and prodded. When I found Boris's number I pressed the button and waited for the ring and the sound of his voice, but neither came. Instead, a different voice told me that the number was no longer in service. A new phone or contract. A better deal. We were no longer linked. Not in the world, nor on social media. I was lost.

Behind the green netting I could make out the bullet holes and shrapnel scars. Soon they too would be erased. Plaster and paint and the past disguised. Attention or inattention. A new phone number and too much time between calls. Too much time. I put the phone in my pocket and began the walk home, as the snow continued to fall.

IV

Islands

For a long time, Charlotte had very little interest in Germany. When she was a child, that country across the ocean represented two things. It was the strange language that her father insisted on speaking with her; one which she understood but pretended not to at the school gates, where she hoped he would switch to English before one of the other kids in her class would notice, storing away this knowledge of something that made Charlotte stand out from the crowd. Germany also represented her grandfather, and the summer vacation trips they made in the 1990s to Berlin, where he lived in the suburb of Lichterfelde. Charlotte hated those trips, and the dark, unpleasant house where her grandfather had created an atmosphere so oppressive she would not even notice that outside the sun was shining high in the sky, and to walk down the garden path to the street beyond felt like an escape. Those trips were always made with her father and her sister, as her mother refused to travel. She would not spend a single moment in the same house as her father-in-law, and Charlotte didn't blame her. Instead, she wondered why her father continued to insist the girls joined him on those trips across the ocean. When they were old enough to choose, old enough to insist, he travelled alone. Not long after, her grandfather died. Charlotte was fifteen when it happened, and was relieved. Not for herself, but for her dad.

'My grandfather was a horrible man,' she said, as we sat in a cafe that looked out across a busy junction, past a shopping centre to the remnants of a Second World War flak tower on the hill beyond. 'He was bitter and racist. He got worse after my grandmother died, everyone always said, but I don't remember how he was then. Only what he was like when he was older. A horrible old man. By the end he spent most of his time just locked up in that house, suspicious of the world and most of the people in it.'

Her grandfather was born in Silesia, the son of a farmer who was the son of a farmer. When the war came, he went off to fight. Afterwards, having survived and returned to his home village, he had only been back at the farm for a matter of weeks when it became clear they were going to have to leave. The borders had shifted. Their house and their fields, the village and the church, the school where her grandfather had taken lessons beneath a portrait of Adolf Hitler, were all now in another country. He was destined to make the journey west alone. His mother died during the war, while he was away at the front. His father, on hearing the news that the farm was to be taken and that they were to be moved, walked out from the kitchen on a Friday evening, just before midnight, and into the woods. He never returned.

Charlotte knew these stories from her own father, who had learned as a child growing up in West Berlin about the fate of his grandparents and his father's cold and hungry journey to a wrecked and twisted, newly divided capital. There, his father worked as a gardener for wealthy families in the suburbs, coming home to a small apartment with sandy soil under his fingernails, which he compared unfavourably with the rich, dark earth that he had left behind 'at home'. Not long after he arrived in Berlin he met Charlotte's grandmother, another refugee and another person alone in the world. This loneliness and the overwhelming nature of the city they found themselves in was all their son could later find to explain how two people, so different, ended up in that small apartment together.

In the late 1950s, as Charlotte's father approached his tenth birthday, the family moved out of the apartment and into the house that Charlotte remembered from her own childhood vacations. In the beginning, things were difficult in the house. Her grandmother tried to create a home for Charlotte's father, and he in turn knew how best to avoid coming into conflict with the man who grew ever more bitter, even now that he had escaped the poky apartment into a house with a garden of its own, as if the sorry patch of lawn and pair of fruit trees offered nothing but a constant reminder of what had been lost. It was around this time that Charlotte's grandfather started travelling to the city centre in the afternoon, after working the gardens, to spend time in the library of the Deutschlandhaus, close to the Wall, and for visits to the nearby pub where his fellow dispossessed used schnapps and dark beer to fuel their dreams of the return, one day, to their homelands. On drinking days, Charlotte's father and grandmother would share a bed, both pretending to be asleep but listening for the sound of stumbling and cursing as it traced a route through the house. Sometimes, the teenage son would tiptoe across the bedroom to turn a key in the door. Only when they heard the sound of snoring through the wall would Charlotte's grandmother return to her own bedroom and climb under the covers alongside her husband.

There were only a few years between the start of the drinking and Charlotte's father becoming old enough to leave the house behind him, but at that age it was an eternity. As the time approached, he plotted his escape. It was not enough simply to leave the house; he also wanted to leave the half-city. He was sick of living on an island. He went to a library around the corner from where he lived, to read travel books and practise his English using old copies of *National Geographic* magazine. He imagined a boat from Hamburg, taking him to Liverpool and then on, across the Atlantic. Or a plane, leaving from Ireland for Iceland and Nova Scotia, before heading down south along the coast. He tried to talk to his mother about his plans, about his hopes and dreams. About how he wanted to take her with him. But she refused to even discuss the subject. Undeterred, he wrote a letter instead, which his father discovered. At the school, his teacher asked him about the black eye and the chipped front tooth, but Charlotte's father knew how he was supposed to answer and he sensed that his teacher was relieved, almost happy not to have to deal with the truth. He tried one more time, not long after he had finished his *Abitur*. He'd applied and been accepted on an apprenticeship scheme for a shipping firm in Hamburg and asked his mother if she would come with him, to make the journey along the transit corridor to the 'mainland' and leave the house and West Berlin behind. There was no chance.

On the day he left, catching a train from Zoo Station, he felt sick with guilt and worry, and although his mother always insisted in letters and phone calls that she was fine, the sickness never left him. Not in Hamburg. Not later, after the company transferred him to Toronto. Not even after he had been back to visit for the first time, taking his wife with him. It did not leave him when his mother died, succumbing to a sickness of her own to achieve what Charlotte's mother called 'her blessed relief'.

'I think he still carries it now,' Charlotte said, 'even after the man is long gone.'

When her grandfather died, her father asked if she or her sister would like to attend the funeral, and surprising herself, Charlotte found she would. Leaving her sister and mother at home, Charlotte and her father flew to Germany and stayed on for a few days to sort out various bureaucratic affairs and things at the house. It was during that trip that Charlotte slowly began to realise that the problem was not Germany. It had been her grandfather. He had poisoned the place for them all: the house, the city and the country. As she helped her father sort through boxes of photographs and paperwork, old clothes and reminders of childhood that her grandmother had squirrelled away in the attic, Charlotte began to talk to her father in his mother tongue. It was hesitant at first, her mouth unused to forming the words she had known since she was a small child. Over those days in the Berlin suburbs, between visits to different offices and sorting through the attic, they went for walks along the old border that had once crossed the bottom of the street, through young forests of slender birch trees and past the facility where American soldiers had practised urban warfare within sight of the East German watchtowers. For the rest of that trip, they only spoke German, and it was like a new part of Charlotte's brain had opened up to her. That summer they came back, as a family, travelling from Berlin to Dresden and the sandstone mountains on the Czech border, over to Leipzig and down to Munich. Germany was no longer that house and her father's childhood. At Lake Constance they took a cabin at a campsite and woke up each morning to the view of the Swiss mountains across the water. They returned to Berlin at the end of the trip and Charlotte began to imagine, for the first time, living in the city.

'And here I am.'

In the course of Charlotte's story, it had gone dark outside. The city beyond the cafe windows had retreated into the gloom, leaving only the reflections of the customers and staff, of their drinks on the tables and the black-and-white photographs on the walls that told the story of the neighbourhood beyond the front door and how much it had changed. Charlotte lived around the corner, and had done so since she arrived in Berlin to start her PhD. To learn more about her neighbourhood, she had joined one of my tours, along with an older couple who were sitting in the cafe with us. Michael and Ruth had also just arrived in the city and were living in the west, close to the Halensee lake and the trade fair grounds. Retired, they were both originally from Manchester, England, but had moved to Israel in the 1950s.

To come to Berlin they had sold their house in Tel Aviv, in a leaving that was, in Ruth's words, a long time coming.

'I cannot imagine we will go back to live,' Ruth said, earlier in the day. 'We'll see how it goes in Berlin. Maybe we'll end up back in England. Who knows. But not to Tel Aviv. I don't think so.'

'For a long time,' Ruth said in the cafe, smiling at Charlotte, 'I also had no interest in Germany.'

At the end of the tour, ten people had come to the cafe, but now it was just the four of us. As Ruth began to talk, Michael wordlessly ordered another round of drinks from the waiter, who was hovering at the end of the bar.

Like Charlotte, Ruth's father was born in Berlin. In Manchester, when Ruth was a child, her father would tell her that the family had always seen themselves as German. They were part of the local community – her grandmother even went to church on a Sunday – and the children went to good schools. They lived in a fine apartment in Schöneberg, and her grandfather's factory in the north of the city was so well known it was namechecked in some of the most popular novels of the 1920s. One of Ruth's great-uncles had been a politician. Another, a famous architect. Apart from her grandmother's churchgoing, none of the family were religious. But of course, her father would say, standing in the kitchen of their semi-detached house in south Manchester, that didn't matter. Not to the Nazis. Her father had seen the situation clearly from the beginning. A young man in 1933, he left Berlin for the final time in February, just a couple of weeks after Hitler came to power. There were family members in London. Some others in Liverpool. He was a young man, with no romantic ties, but he did leave his parents and the rest of his family behind. Later, he would try and explain to Ruth why even those who had the chance to leave, which was by no means most, didn't follow him out of the country. There were many reasons; but for his parents, they simply believed there was no chance this situation was going to continue, there was no way it could last, until it was too late. Some members of his family did manage to follow him over. One of Ruth's cousins was on the *Kindertransport*, arriving at Liverpool Street station. But the rest didn't. They were loaded onto trains of a different kind, put there by people they still saw as their fellow countrymen. The trains took them south and east. Theresienstadt. Treblinka. Auschwitz. Germans killed by Germans, for being Jews.

'So you can understand why I had very little interest in Germany, as a young woman,' Ruth continued. It was strange, she said, but her father had not felt the same way about the country. He had returned to the land of his birth many times. He still enjoyed speaking German, still read his favourite books. He loved Thomas Mann especially. He even went to Poland, to see those places with his own eyes, those terrible places, and say his goodbyes. Later, after Michael and Ruth had moved to Israel, he would travel to visit them via Berlin. The city was divided then, of course, but he still had friends on either side of the border that would later become the Berlin Wall. After the Wall was built, he would tell his grandchildren in Israel stories of the Friedrichstraße station that sounded like episodes from a spy novel.

Michael also went to Germany at that time, Ruth said, nodding in the direction of her husband. Mainly for work, for conferences in Heidelberg and Göttingen, a trip behind the Wall to Weimar and then again, later, after the Wall was long gone. But Ruth couldn't do it. She couldn't face it. For decades she refused, she simply refused.

They had German friends, she continued. One couple especially, who they met during a year when Michael was based in the United States, in Washington DC. Heiner and Ute, from Munich. Ruth said their names with a smile. They loved skiing, and had an apartment in Garmisch-Partenkirchen. They said that Michael and Ruth could use it whenever they liked. In the States, the two couples took many trips together. To Manhattan for the theatre, or up into Maine or Vermont for the skiing. Later, Heiner and Ute travelled to Tel Aviv. Michael drove the four of them to Jerusalem. They went to Yad Vashem. That was how close the two couples were. That Heiner and Ute felt able to go, and that Michael and Ruth felt able to take them.

'And yet, here you are,' Charlotte said.

Ruth sipped her beer.

'Heiner had a birthday party,' she said, putting her glass carefully back down on the table in front of her. It was to be held at their house, in Munich. Of course, Ruth and Michael had been invited many times before, and she had always politely refused. Heiner and Ute understood completely, but this was his seventieth and he really wanted them to be there. It was Michael who came up with a plan and made Ruth an offer. Heiner and Ute's house was barely twenty minutes from Munich airport. They could fly in, take a taxi, go to the party and fly out again. They wouldn't be going to *Germany*. They would be going to Heiner and Ute's. That was how he phrased it.

In the cafe, Michael nodded his agreement.

But then, Ruth said, she thought to herself: no. If they were going to do it, to make that step, then they were going to do it properly. Instead of twenty-four hours, they booked a trip of five days. They went to the party and they went into Munich. They caught a train to the foothills of the Alps and they went to Dachau. A year later, they returned to visit Hamburg. And a year after that, Berlin. For Ruth, it was the third trip that was different. In Munich and Hamburg it had been uncomfortable, difficult even. To take that first step onto German soil. But in Berlin, she did not feel uncomfortable at all. This was her father's city, and she felt it immediately: this was a homecoming. It had been taken away from him, but now she could take it back.

One of the first places they visited was Grunewald station, where Ruth's grandparents had been put onto the trains. And then they went to the house in Schöneberg, making the return journey that her grandparents were never able to make. Outside the front door two brass cobblestones had been laid in the pavement, one for each of them. It was a shock to Ruth to see their names looking up at her. She hadn't known these *Stolpesteine*, these stumbling stones, had been laid. Later, she discovered they had been sponsored by another branch of the family, her father's cousins, who they had lost contact with over the years. Ruth could still remember kneeling down on the pavement and wiping the tiny memorials clean with her handkerchief. Some people didn't like these stones, she said. They didn't like them because people could walk on them. Because dogs could do their business on them. But Ruth didn't feel like that. Once she got over the shock of the discovery, she realised she was happy. It might seem like an odd emotion, she said to us in the cafe, but it was certainly happiness that she felt. She was sadly happy, and that was the only way she could think to describe it, because although they had been taken away, forced to leave their home and everything they knew, forced onto those cattle trucks and into those camps, although they had suffered and ultimately been murdered, they could not be completely erased. They were still there, in Berlin. They still belonged to the city. And at that moment, kneeling on the pavement, Ruth had realised that she did too.

The cafe shrank back as Ruth spoke, as we were taken with her, away from that place and into her story. As we walked along the street together earlier something similar had happened, as Ruth traced our route on a map she held all afternoon, waiting for the moment we reached the spot where her grandfather's factory had once stood. Although I was leading this mixed group of people through the neighbourhood, telling them the stories of an old village beyond the city limits, where witches had been burned and where sandy paths through the meadows and birch forests linked the farmsteads and windmills with the city beyond, telling them the stories of the arrival of industry and the rapid growth, the devastation of war and the post-industrial present, Ruth was listening, but she was not seeing my version of the neighbourhood. She was seeing another, remembered from her childhood and her father's tales of these streets. She was seeing the neighbourhood through his eyes, as he visited his father's factory, back when the whole place was loud and polluted, filled with twice as many people as would live there almost a century later, on the day we took our walk.

The city retreated in her gaze as she travelled back in time. She did not see the litter or the dog shit or the abandoned sofa. She did not hear Michael, as he effortlessly translated the Arabic sign above a travel agents, comparing what was written with the very different German version printed alongside. In those moments, Ruth was not with us in this neighbourhood, the place where Charlotte had just moved to and where K. and I lived in our apartment on the top floor. She was standing, instead, on a street lined with recounted memories, a place she had never before visited but had seen many times, conjured from her father's stories and the handful of photographs he had taken with him to England.

'There,' she said to me, looking down at her map in one hand as she grabbed my arm with the other. The rest of the group were taking photographs of a mural beside the railway lines, but she was pointing at a nondescript apartment block. It had been built in the 1980s, with a Croatian restaurant and a hairdressers on the ground floor. Beyond was the tower of the old crematorium, now an art space, and the red-brick walls of the post office, built during Ruth's father's childhood.

We looked at the apartment block and tried to imagine the factory. The men at the gates. The sound of the machines. The smoke from the chimneys. During his apprenticeship, her father would have approached those gates each and every morning. One day it would have been his. In another world.

I asked her if he had ever received compensation. After the war. Or whether she had.

Ruth shrugged.

'Maybe he was offered it,' she said. 'I don't know. He wouldn't have taken it anyway.'

From there we walked through the streets to the viewing platform atop the old flak tower, looking out across the north of the city.

'It seems so big,' Charlotte said, and shivered. 'Like you can't see out.'

There were a couple of her fellow researchers at the university who boasted that it was months since they had left the city limits. As if it was still an island, like it had been for her father.

'You should go out,' Michael said, his voice soft. 'It's very easy. You can do it on the train. Or rent a bike. Berlin's not as big as you think. There's no need to think of it as an island. Not if you don't want to.'

Outside the cafe, we said our goodbyes. Ruth and Michael crossed the street to the S-Bahn station, while Charlotte and I walked away, following the street down the hill, past the parade of call-shops and euro-stores, kebab restaurants, pawnbrokers and bookmakers.

'Do you ever get homesick?' Charlotte asked

She had pulled her coat tightly around her, looking ahead to chart a path through the pedestrians bottlenecked outside a Turkish supermarket as she asked the question.

I told her I wasn't sure.

'I miss people,' she said. 'But also places. I miss knowing how things work. How to make things work.'

'Sometimes I think I'm homesick for Berlin.'

She looked at me. I tried to explain what I meant. That I missed the city I had known before. The people and the places. Exactly as she did, with Toronto and Canada, but here, without having moved more than a few streets north from where I first landed.

'That's nostalgia,' Charlotte said. 'You're just getting old. Things change and you don't like it. It's normal, but you are not homesick for Berlin. You're homesick for your youth.'

I had to concede that she might be right.

We said goodbye at the corner. It was a short distance to the apartment, but as I walked I imagined turning on my heel instead, going back up the street, past the cafe and the shopping centre, the flak tower and the park, until I met the route of the Berlin Wall, following it until it intersected with our old street, the one in earshot of the church bells, where I lived with K. after Tomas died and she opened her door to me and I never left. In front of the apartment building was a shiny brass cobblestone. I hadn't thought about in a long, long time, and yet I had seen it every time I arrived or left that apartment. As Ruth had been speaking in the cafe earlier, I had seen the shiny cobblestone once more. A small collection of words and numbers.

Here lived
Ephraim Worrmann
Born 1878
Deported 1943
Murdered at Auschwitz

Once, when I left the apartment, I saw someone had rested a white flower against the wall. The stumbling stone seemed shinier, too, as if recently polished. For a while, Ephraim Worrmann had lived in the same house as us. He would have heard the same church bells and the same sound of footsteps on the same paving stones, echoing beneath his window, as we heard beneath ours, decades later.

K. was already home when I got back to the apartment, sitting in the kitchen, reading on her phone. She told me I looked pale. I asked her when she had last walked past our old apartment. It had been a few weeks before, on her way to meet a friend at the flea market.

'Had anything changed?'

She asked me what I meant. I reminded her about the motorbike our neighbour drove. Maybe he had upgraded to a new model? Or the kindergarten across the street and the restaurant at the end of the road, where we had watched the World Cup on a big screen. Were they both still there? What about Ephraim's stone? Was *that* still there? Had anyone taken time to polish it recently? Or left a fresh flower?

She tried to answer the questions, and then asked me again if I was all right.

I wasn't sure. I went through to the living room and sat down on the couch, the lights of the city shining beneath a dark, cloud-covered sky. When I saw Ephraim's stone for the first time, I had tried to imagine the journey. From our old street and our old house, to Große Hamburger Straße and a school transformed into an internment centre. To Grunewald station and onto the trains. Across the river and into occupied lands. To Auschwitz. I had tried to imagine the journey but, although I could picture all the places, there was no way. I failed. Of course I failed. I had all the information, but I couldn't possibly know.

V

Die Toten mahnen uns

When her grandmother died, K. used the small inheritance to buy a camera. From then on, she took it almost everywhere she went in case she stumbled across something to add to her collection. Back then, K. rarely photographed people. Instead, she was interested in memory. In grand statues and hastily painted murals. In memorials, official and unofficial. In faded slogans spray-painted on walls and ghost signs on gable ends. She visited cemeteries and walked the lines of headstones in granite and marble, a series of names and dates, biblical quotations and messages left by the living for the dead. In Wilmersdorf, she captured a bicycle, painted white and chained to the railings of a bridge over the canal. On Alexanderplatz, she discovered a collection of red candles and scattered flowers. A few weeks later she found the candles and the flowers had been cleared away, but her photographs remained.

Every month or so, she downloaded her images onto a laptop and set up the projector in the living room. Her

photographs were beamed onto the white wall we shared
with the neighbours, and K. began the editing process,
choosing which ones to keep, which ones to work on, and
which to discard. When friends learned of K.'s new hobby,
they presumed it must be linked to her work in the History
department of the university, but it wasn't. Her photographs,
she said, were a place free of all the conditions and competing
motivations and pressures that her work life placed on her.
They were for her and her alone.

'An antidote to academia,' is what she called it.

One of the places she returned to on numerous occasions,
to capture different weather conditions or times of day,
was the Dorotheenstadt cemetery. She went there to collect
the writers: the graves of Brecht and Weigel, within sight
of their old house on Chauseestraße; Christa Wolf and the
jam jar filled with pens, left by her fans; Heinrich Mann, his
headstone slowly being swallowed by the bush that grew
around it. Mann was originally buried in California, at the
end of his long exile, having died as he prepared to leave the
United States for the fledgling German Democratic Republic.
A decade later, the East Germans finally got their man as his
remains were exhumed and brought to Berlin for reburial. In
that same year, as well as his headstone, the authorities started
work on something else: a Wall to divide the city, that passed
only a few hundred metres from where Mann now lay.

Heinrich Mann was K.'s grandmother's favourite writer,
even more so than his Nobel-prize-winning brother Thomas.
After she died, and in the days before the funeral, we
travelled to her apartment in the south of the city, close to the
Botanical Gardens, to help K.'s parents clear it out. We should
take anything we wanted, K.'s father said, his eyes heavy

with grief. We did not take much. A porcelain jug and a set of schnapps glasses that reminded K. of Christmas as a small child. A particular kitchen knife and some photographs to hang in our bedroom. And her Mann collection. The novels and essays, the biographies and collected works. Thomas and Heinrich, Erika and Klaus. We gathered the books in cotton shopping bags to take them home, where we cleared an entire shelf to house them all together. That evening, as we looked through them, sitting on the floor beside the bookshelf, we discovered the books were filled with tiny writing in the margins, notes made by K.'s grandmother for no reason other than her own interest, and made with no expectation that they would ever be read. In those commentaries, she explored the themes and the storyline, the settings and the characters. She made comparisons with other works and notes on the writing style.

As we read them, we could hear her voice once more.

K.'s grandmother was laid to rest in a forest cemetery not far from where K. grew up. The music was Beethoven and Tchaikovsky, and her ashes were lowered into an unmarked grave. She had no wish for a headstone. Instead, she wanted to be remembered in our minds and through the photographs and letters she had been happy to pass on. We liked to think she would enjoy that we could still argue with her opinions, scribbled in the margins of her beloved books. Her funeral was held in the shade of the cemetery, the air oppressive with late summer heat. Later, during the wake at K.'s parents' house, we excused ourselves to walk in the forest, following the route through the trees that her grandmother had taken an excited young girl on nearly three decades before, dodging mosquitoes on their way to the lake.

There was no one on the shore or in the water when we got there, so we stripped down to nothing and cooled ourselves, naked in the deep waters, surrounded by trees.

When K. and I got together, three of her grandparents were still alive. Now, they were all gone. In the winter that followed her grandmother's death, we watched as protests gathered pace across the country, against the media and the influence of Islam, against the government's refugee policies and the European project. K. was worried. At work she studied the period between the wars, and the years that led Europe from the muddy trenches of Flanders to the extermination camps. Increasingly, she said, we only had the dead to remind us of those times. There were not many left who could look us in the eye and tell us what they saw, tell us with their own voices and memories what they experienced. If there was no one left to remember, she continued, it became all too easy to forget.

Over that winter, as German flags flew beneath the Dresden night sky alongside appropriated symbols of resistance, crude caricatures of the German Chancellor and slogans accusing the media of lying to ordinary people, K. took me to Dorotheenstadt. As she photographed the Mann grave, crowned with a dusting of snow, I thought about the afternoons we had spent with her grandparents and the stories they had told. Of growing up in the period that was now their granddaughter's field of expertise; of childhood friends who disappeared once the fighting started, never to return; of Soviet prison camps and long marches; and of classmates who were sent east to fight and were never heard of again.

K. pulled aside leaves and brushed away snow, to find the small, sorrowful adjunct to Heinrich Mann's grave. It was a plaque, dedicated to the memory of his wife, Nelly Kröger. She had died before him, while they were still in their American exile, by taking an overdose of sleeping pills. Nelly was buried in Santa Monica, and when Heinrich was brought home they left her there, the woman whom Heinrich had met when she was working as a hostess in a Berlin bar, and the woman he fell in love with and married, despite the disapproval of the rest of the Mann family. In one of the biographies on our shelves there was a quote from her brother-in-law Thomas, the prize-winner, describing Nelly as a *Schreckliche Trulle*.

A frightful trollop.

She sounds like a lot of fun, K.'s grandmother had written, in her small, neat handwriting, alongside the text.

That January we got up early on a Sunday morning to catch the U-Bahn south to Alexanderplatz. As we changed trains in the catacombs beneath the station, the number of people around us increased. Outside the ground was icy and the wind whipped viciously along the city streets. Our fellow passengers wore heavy overcoats and hats. Some carried flagpoles wrapped in red fabric. Others held red carnations in gloved hands. Our destination was another cemetery, where the crowds were gathering to remember Karl Liebknecht and Rosa Luxemburg, the red carnations to be left on the stones that carried their names. From the station we followed the line of people to the memorial site, as music played and political rhetoric drifted out via megaphone into the frozen air. There were many graves and memorials alongside those for Karl and Rosa, and the size of the respective piles of carnations offered a floristic, historical judgement on the legacies of Ernst Thälmann and Walter Ulbricht, Otto Grotewohl and Wilhelm Pieck. K. placed her own on the large pile that almost completely covered Rosa Luxemburg's grave, as a man dressed as Lenin stood on the steps of the memorial with his arms folded and observed the scene through narrowed eyes.

Die Toten mahnen uns

The dead remind us. On a summer day we waited at Zoo Station for the train. It was almost a year since K.'s grandmother died. The protests in Dresden seemed to have petered out, but there were other forces gathering, on the streets and in election campaigns. On the platform at Zoo, the mood was light. Bags had been filled for a day at the lake. Cyclists pushed their bikes through the crowd to find the best spot. Groups of walkers and families loaded with all the paraphernalia for a picnic waited patiently for the S-Bahn to arrive. It was a classic Berlin warm-weather exodus, to the woods and the water, whether within the city limits or without.

We all squeezed aboard when the train arrived, and from where we stood we could look out across the western districts of the city as it made its way towards our destination. We climbed down from the train at Grunewald and its colony of villas, where Christopher Isherwood once taught English to spoiled rich-kids and where the winners of Berlin's industrialisation escaped the pollution and harsh realities of the city they had helped create, to this place beneath the gloomy pines. It was not far, geographically, from the suburb where K. had grown up, but this neighbourhood around the station felt grand in a way that the West Berlin neighbourhood of her childhood never would. We queued at the bakery for bread rolls and bottles of water. Across the square, a couple carried their bags of shopping home from the supermarket. An older man sat on a bench, enjoying an ice cream that dripped onto his pastel-blue shirt. He didn't seem to care.

We followed signs that guided us around the side of the station building, and up a slight incline until we were once again level with the tracks. The signs had led us to a platform at which trains no longer called, a platform that maintained its number but had a very different purpose. It had been to Platform 17 at Grunewald station that Berlin's Jews were taken, from Mitte and Friedrichshain, the tenement blocks around Alexanderplatz and the villas of Grunewald. Fifty thousand Jews, interned and deported, loaded onto the trains for Theresienstadt and Łódź, Breslau and Auschwitz. As we walked along, each transport was listed at the edge of the platform, the destinations and the numbers of people deported. I thought about Ephraim Worrmann, who had lived in our old apartment building long before us and who was murdered in Auschwitz. I searched the list along the platform for deportations in the year he had been taken.

12.3.1943 / 944 JUDEN / BERLIN-AUSCHWITZ

That could have been his train, the departure point and destination listed so simply, like any train from here to there, and yet loaded with meaning. It could have been his train, but there were many others too. A whole line of them.

The list of transports ran the entire length of Platform 17, along both sides. For some, the numbers were small. Ten on this train. Seventeen on the next. As the Holocaust progressed, the numbers grew larger, running into the thousands. Stones had been left along the edge of the platform, as family members and friends commemorated certain trains. A young family joined us on the platform, and we listened as the father attempted to explain to his six-year-old daughter what it was we were all looking at. But we were struggling to comprehend it ourselves, this story of people and trains and gas chambers and the worst places on earth, and it was hard to imagine how he was going to bring this across to a young child. He did his best. The dead remind us. Listen, and repeat.

We left Platform 17 behind us, to follow an old forester's track through the woods, past the sand dunes and the waterworks to the lake that stood in the shadow of a huge rubble mountain, built with the debris of war and topped with the crumbling domes of an abandoned American Listening Station. That was the Devil's Mountain, and the cool waters belonged to the Devil's Lake. As children, K. and her schoolmates had traded stories about the lake, of the creatures that lived in its depths and the mysterious princess who tempted children to the water's edge with the promise of treasures beyond the imagination, but who was no princess at all.

'I would only swim there with my grandmother or my parents around,' K. said. The stories they heard were always about kids who had gone there alone.

We sat down on the grass by the lake, among the nudists and the other sun-worshippers. When we had been there after K.'s grandmother's funeral we had been alone, in our thoughts and our memories and in the water, but on that summer weekend there were hundreds of people in the tall grass, on the beach and in the lake. K. produced two beers from her backpack and we sat in the sun for a while. We watched the swimmers and listened to three naked men arguing where they were sitting on a fallen tree. A gust of wind caught a newspaper just right, and scattered the supplements in different directions. A young boy pissed against a tree, hands on hips, his trunks around his ankles.

The fragments of memory.

We went down into the water, swimming out alongside each other from the beach to the centre of the lake and a floating platform. K. got there first, holding onto the platform with one hand as I slowed to a breaststroke as I approached her. Later, I could always conjure up her face in that moment, eyes blinking away the water as it ran from her hair and down across her face. She had caught the sun. As I reached her we kissed. Her lips were cold and tasted of the lake. We climbed onto the platform and allowed ourselves to dry in the sun. The sound of the children playing in the shallows was carried across the water to us, mingling with the sound of birds and the rustle of trees as they moved in the sporadic summer breeze. As the platform rocked gently in the centre of the lake, I knew that this was one of those moments that would stay. Despite starting the morning at Platform 17 and all the stories that lingered there beside the rusting railway tracks, this moment that came after, on the lake and in the sunshine, feeling K.'s body against mine as we sat there, was to be one of my happiest Berlin memories. Shielding my eyes from the sunshine, I looked at K. and reached out to squeeze her hand. She was smiling. I asked her what she was thinking about.

'My Oma,' she said.

The lake continued to hold no fear for K., because her grandmother was still with us.

It was funny, she continued, tracing a pattern in the water that had formed a puddle around us where we sat, but it seemed easier there, floating on the lake, to think of her. To talk to her. When K. was there, in the forest or on the slopes of Devil's Mountain, sitting on the beach or swimming across the lake, one of the first things she would always think about was her grandmother. Because that was their place.

We continued to talk about the rest of the day, as we planned our return walk through the woods and the S-Bahn that would take us home. We would go to the pub, stopping for a kebab at the stand by the station, the smell of mosquito spray, sun cream and lake water lingering on our skin. In the pub I would read a day-old newspaper while K. pulled a book from her bag, and we would sit in silence, content. On the way home she would tell me another story of her grandmother, another memory prompted by the upcoming anniversary of her grandmother's death and our trip to the lake. Back at the apartment, she would call her father, and then we would go to bed, a lazy, gentle closeness via our fingertips, no clothes and no sheets, because the weather hadn't yet broken and in that bedroom under the roof it was simply too hot for anything else.

From the floating platform we could see three teenage boys approaching. Our peace would soon be disturbed by the spray of *Arschbombe* and skinny-armed macho posturing.

As the first of the boys made it to the platform and reached for the metal ladder, K. stood and dived in over his head, a graceful re-entry into the coolness of the lake, swimming one, two, three strokes beneath the surface before she emerged to strike for the shore. I watched her swim away, the platform wobbling beneath me as the boys found their feet. The weeping willows brushed the surface of the lake on the far side. Dragonflies buzzed in the area beyond the buoys, where no one was supposed to swim. Swallows in the sky. A dog, causing chaos in the shallows. The Devil's Lake. Their place. Our place. As the boys debated exactly how they were going leap and plunge into its depths, I slid off the platform into the cold water, following K., who had by now almost reached the shore.

VI

Dacha

Markus could remember clearly the day they first set eyes on what would become their small patch of forest. It started with an invitation from the Ministry, although there had been whispers in the halls and canteens, both in Markus's department and elsewhere, for months. When the invitation arrived, it became clear the whispers had been true: comrades of a certain level and above were to be granted a patch of land in the forest, about an hour from Berlin and allocated to the Ministry by the military for the purposes of rest and recuperation. The chosen comrades could choose a dacha to be built on the land, a summer cabin, from a range of prefabricated models, and create their own garden beneath the slender pines. There was a nominal annual rent to pay, to cover water and refuse collection, but ultimately it was a reward for their work and recognition of their status and what they had done for the Ministry, the Party and for socialism.

The invitation arrived via the Ministry's internal mail system in the April of 1981, along with a ground plan of the colony that had been carved out of a section of forest curled around the shore of a lake. A comrade's position in the Ministry dictated not only whether they received an invitation in the first place, but also where on the ground plan their property had been allocated. The patch allocated to Markus and his wife, Clara, was coloured indigo, while all the rest were white. It was about two unnamed streets from the lake shore. The waterfront properties, he presumed, had been allocated to men more important than him. He did not mind too much. Loyal as he was, he did not need to see his boss over the garden fence during his weekends off.

The following Saturday Markus and Clara drove out from Berlin in their Wartburg. It was possible to take the train, but Markus wanted to test how long it took to drive. Clara had packed a picnic, as the ground plan indicated there was a bathing beach open to all residents of the colony. Being April, it was too cold for swimming, but she imagined sitting on the sand in their bare feet, with their bread rolls and a view across the calm waters of the lake. As it happened, when they got there, turning off the main road and following a dirt track criss-crossed with tree roots and rutted from the construction vehicles, the beach was not ready yet. It was being used as a car park for the diggers and trucks, with a temporary cabin for the workers and the architects. Nor were most of the cabins ready. Markus and Clara's dacha was still piled on the back of a truck, although the concrete foundation upon which it would be erected had already been poured. Being Sunday, no one was working on the site, but they felt no impatience; there was no hurry. Markus and Clara were in their early thirties. He was doing well at the Ministry. She was a successful employee of the local housing association in their district. This was going to be their place for many summers to come.

And so, they stood, where later they would erect an entrance gate to the property, and lay a cracked flagstone path leading through the immaculate lawn to the veranda. It was there that Markus would build, over the course of one summer, an outdoor kitchen with grill and bread oven, and the pool that would be added in the 1990s to replace the vegetable patch that made no sense once Clara's knees started to cause her problems and, in any case, everything was much cheaper nowadays at the supermarket that had opened on the edge of the closest village. On that April day it was all for the future. Markus stood and looked at the empty space where his dacha would stand, and considered it his just reward. He worked hard, selflessly and diligently for the Ministry. It had cost him friendships and strained relationships within the family, especially on Clara's side. But this place among the trees was a symbol of what made it all worthwhile, a gesture of gratitude from those for whom he worked. The people, of course. And their representatives.

It was his favourite place on earth, Markus told me, on more than one occasion, as we sat in Franz's pub. He would talk about the colony and the sound of the summer along its rutted dirt lanes. Conversation from gardens drifting across the neatly trimmed hedges. The bike bells and the splash of bodies hitting the water, down on the beach. The noise of the forest at night, as the animals moved beyond the back fence. He told me how the colony had changed, especially in the years after the Wall came down. He and Clara had been allowed to keep the dacha under the old conditions, but they would not be allowed to pass the contract on. So, as his old colleagues died off or moved away, the military sold off the small parcels of land as they became available. Young families took them over. Wealthy Berliners who quickly tore down the old, prefabricated cabins and replaced them with small, modernist villas that could be heated in the winter and used all year round. On the beach a kiosk opened, selling beers and boiled sausages, ice creams and inflatable toys. The campground was given permission to expand down the lakeshore, right up to the first of the colony houses. But some things remained the same. Despite appeals from the new landowners, the roads between the properties remained sandy tracks, and only the largest of potholes prompted a road crew to drive out from the nearby town and into the woods. And the young people of the colony continued to meet, on the paths and down on the beach, as they always had done, as the children of the new landowners and the grandchildren of the long-pensioned Ministry employees built friendships in the shallows.

'My favourite place,' Markus repeated, and then laughed. 'It shouldn't be a surprise. We have always loved the forest. For thousands of years. It's long been our place of escape, our sanctuary.'

'Ever since Hermann,' I said.

'Exactly. Ever since Hermann.'

Markus talked more about his dacha in the woods, and spent more time there, after Otto died and Konrad disappeared. The simplest of questions could trigger another story, an anecdote twice-removed or a memory. They were all there in his mind, neatly archived and waiting to be triggered, yet he rarely repeated himself. There were more than enough to be going on with.

A few months after that April day when they had cast their eyes over the construction site and imagined all they would create there beneath the pines, Markus travelled to Potsdam to visit his father, Klaus. Klaus lived in a *Plattenbau* concrete-slab apartment block close to Babelsberg Palace, and Markus visited him once a month to go for a walk in the park. Because of a particularly time-intensive case he had been working on, Markus had missed a few months, and he hadn't told his father about the dacha in the woods. He gave Klaus the news as they stood on the crest of the hill, a spot with a view down into Potsdam in one direction, and across the watchtowers and the no man's land of the border with West Berlin in the other. When Markus told Klaus about the planned dacha, the forest and the name of the lake, it was the latter his father asked him to repeat. When he said it again, Klaus looked at him for a moment and then turned away, walking back down the path towards the park gate without a word. Markus hurried to follow him down the hill, having to trot as if they had gone back in time to Markus's childhood as he followed his father on walks through the iron ore mountains south of Leipzig, or along the promenades of Baltic resorts.

Markus caught up with him only when they reached the pub on the corner, close to Klaus's apartment. It was early afternoon and they were the only customers. The barman knew Klaus, and he knew the son. He knew that Klaus was a Party man in Potsdam and that the son worked for the Ministry in Berlin. These were important men, and yet in that pub, the barman and the regulars treated Klaus and Markus like anyone else. Which was, Klaus always told his son, exactly how it should be. But on that day, Markus found Klaus sitting at a table with his back to the wall, looking down at his hands that were fidgeting with a box of matches. The barman, unbidden, brought over two glasses of dark beer, dropping two beer mats from the side of his hand onto the polished surface of the table, before placing the beers on top of them.

Klaus lit a cigarette. He had the lined face of an old smoker, but Markus read in his father's face not the lines of a pack a day, but the story of his father's early life; the story of war. Markus was born in 1947, two years into the peace, when his father was just twenty-four. To Markus, Klaus had always had lines on his face, as he stood there at the gates, waiting to collect his son after those first kindergarten classes in Potsdam. His father looked old, his friends told him in high school, and they never believed Markus when he told them Klaus's true age. As Markus got older still, he began to imagine that what he could see in his father was not the story of one war, but of all the wars. The trenches of World War I and the eastern front of World War II. The Franco-Prussian battles and the bloodshed of the Thirty Years War. Back to Hermann and the defeat of the Romans in the Teutoburg Forest. Klaus was barely in his twenties when the war ended, and yet in his son's eyes he was and would always be an old soldier. The oldest of soldiers, determined that his fight should be the last.

Later, when he told me the story of that day in Potsdam, he could still smell his father's cigarette as they sat there in the pub. He could still taste the beer and hear the sound of the barman's footsteps as he walked back to his usual place behind the counter. Klaus smoked and sipped, while his son sat opposite him and waited. Then Klaus began to speak. He began to speak of those April days in 1945 and the long, desperate retreat through boglands, meadows and forests east of Berlin in the face of the approaching Red Army. He spoke of trying to dodge the Brownshirts, who roamed the countryside even though everyone knew the war was lost, looking for deserters and other traitors to kill. Those they found were executed on the side of the road, and hung from the nearest tree as a warning to others.

Klaus and a friend had deserted. They decided together that they had not survived this long to be killed in the final battle of a futile war that should have long been over. They decided they were going to go home to their families, and find warmth and hope in the only place it seemed possible there was any left.

As he sat in that Potsdam bar and told his son the story, one which Markus had never heard before, Klaus closed his eyes. He was picturing everything as he spoke, a movie reel spooled behind his eyelids. He could see the muddy tracks as they avoided the main roads with their columns of refugees trudging between a dishonour guard of bodies swinging in the trees. He could feel the ill-fitting peasant clothes, stolen from an abandoned farmhouse when they decided to remove their uniforms. He could smell the smoke of the battlefield getting ever closer, mingling with the scent of a springtime that was going to happen anyway, whatever the humans decided to do to each other in what felt, to them, like an eternal winter.

He remembered one scene vividly, Markus said. He told him how Klaus and his friend came upon a farmhouse on the edge of a village. They had only just avoided a patrol and still had the sound of gunshots, aimed at less fortunate souls, ringing in their ears. The farmhouse was surrounded by flowers, in the beds around the lawn and in window boxes along the first-floor balcony. In that moment, as they stood in the lane and looked across the garden to this house, colourful and untroubled, it was as if nothing was happening. There was a woman in the garden, wearing a white dress, with a basket over her arm. Klaus could see her, fifty years later, and remembered the urgency in his voice as he told her to leave. She was the most beautiful woman he ever saw, he told Markus, perhaps for his friend as well. They both continued to talk to her, trying to persuade her that she had to leave. She could not wait. She had to leave and keep going. But the woman smiled and shook her head. She went back into the farmhouse. Later, Klaus would not only wonder what happened to her, but whether he had imagined her. It was the same question Markus asked him in the Potsdam pub, as they ordered another round of beers.

What of his friend? Couldn't he have confirmed whether the woman was real or not? But it was not possible. The next day, as they moved through the forest, close to a glistening lake, Klaus heard a bang. And then another. He stumbled forward, wondering why he could not move as he had been

PAUL SCRATON

only moments before, and then he felt the pain. It was his right leg. The journey from feeling nothing, feeling normal, to the scorching intensity of what he now experienced had taken a matter of seconds and left him breathless. He fell forward, into a patch of ferns and brambles, half-swallowed by the mossy forest floor. He heard voices and closed his eyes. Later, those voices would return to him. Sometimes they spoke German. Other times, Russian. They returned so often, he was no longer sure he truly remembered the scene. It didn't matter. He lay there, feeling the pain in a way that he had never felt anything before, realising that although he had never felt more alive than he did at that moment, if he was to survive, he had to be dead. The voices retreated. He lay there a little longer, counting in his head. First to a hundred, then to two hundred. How many footsteps in the undergrowth? Another hundred. How far out of earshot would they be now? A few hundred more. And then he sat up.

He had been shot in the leg, but apart from a slight limp that would develop much later in life, he had been lucky. His friend had not. Klaus found him a few metres away, face down. The ferns had already begun to curl around his body and the moss was stained with blood. Klaus dug at it, revealing the sandy soil below. He dug a little more, with his hands and his mess tin. He knew he had to leave, but he had to finish this first. A shallow grave for his best friend. They had known each other since school and been called up together. They had fought and been scared and deserted together. He buried his friend in the forest because there was nothing else he could do, and he left him there for the same reason. When he reached the next village he came to a place where Clara and Markus would later buy oranges

88

from Spain and tomatoes from Italy, to take with them to their dacha in the woods, and Klaus slipped into a refugee column and caught one of the final transports to Berlin. A month later, the war was over. Klaus had survived. His best friend was still lying in the woods.

'You should come and visit us,' Markus would say to me in the pub when the subject of the dacha came up. He told us that we could stay at the campground and come to their dacha for a barbecue. We could walk in the woods and swim in the lake. Escape the city for a while. Understand why it was that he loved the place so much. But K. was not keen. It was not the idea of the place, the forest or the lake, but Markus. She had never warmed to him. It was not because of how he was, how he acted with her, or me in the pub, but what he had been. His work at the Ministry. Those five letters.

STASI.

In the pub we could speak about these things, especially in the later years, because Markus enjoyed talking and because I drank enough to have the courage to ask. Not about what he did, in that office in Lichtenberg and on the streets and in the safe houses. Not the things that earned him the commendations that by definition had to remain private and which led him to that dacha in the woods. But I was interested in his motivations. Not so much the 'what' but the 'why'. We had that conversation a number of times in the years Markus and I knew each other, and the answer was slightly different each time. After all, he didn't like repeating himself.

✳

When Klaus arrived in Berlin after the war, the city was home to destruction that spoke of the violent collapse of an entire empire. In that city named for the swamp it was built upon, a place where its whole history was the taming the nature of the place and creating order among the marshlands and riverbanks, Klaus picked his way through the rubble past an endless parade of devastated buildings and wondered whether it was worth rebuilding. Let the swamp reclaim it.

In those early months after the war ended, Klaus felt the effects of an apocalyptic atmosphere that had engulfed the city. He heard of the phantom railway worker who murdered passengers as they travelled alone along suburban train lines, and then had sex with the corpse. He read the newspaper articles about lakes filled with the bodies of women raped by Red Army soldiers and who had committed suicide. Among the wreckage of the Anhalter station, he witnessed the gathering of ever more refugees from the East. The Prussian landowner, with nothing to his name but the wooden trolley he pulled behind him. The Silesian farmer, staring wide-eyed at the ravaged city beyond the station platforms, the dark soil of his homeland still visible beneath his nails. The other characters, as they moved slowly through the dark and gloomy shadows of the station, the housewives on their way to the pump for water and the parade of broken soldiers, returning from the front.

And yet, for Klaus there remained hope.

In those early months, in the autumn of 1945, he went to a play in Kreuzberg. Brecht. Despite the destruction of much of the city centre and the poverty experienced by its defeated residents, the theatregoers did their best, stepping out in as fine clothes as they could muster to take their seats in front of the stage. For Klaus, it felt like an act that represented the slow return of freedom to Berlin, part of the liberation of the city. It was a statement that normalcy could return to these streets. In this city, at that time, it was almost revolutionary.

It was during this period, Markus said, that his father became a Communist. He would later tell his son that his politics were a direct result of the brutality and totality of defeat, but it was more than that. It was about what he had experienced during the war and, most of all, those days in the forest. In an old library book, Klaus found a picture of Käthe Kollwitz's famous painting, *Nie wieder Krieg*. She had told them, but they had not listened. Now they would. It was how he brought Markus up. Never again war. And only socialism, Klaus told his son, could bring a true peace. It was, of course, not just that. It wasn't only what had happened in Berlin, or the traumas they had experienced. It was also what had been done elsewhere. In the towns and the villages. In the camps. Those things done in the name of Germany. In his name, and on his behalf. Socialism was the only answer. Klaus was sure of it. It was why he joined the Party, and why he was proud when Markus joined the Ministry. They were building socialism on German soil. They were building peace. Never again war.

All nations need their founding myths.

By the 1980s, Markus was no longer sure what his father thought about the socialism they had built and fought for. From that day in Potsdam, Klaus's attention shifted. An engineer after the war, illness had forced him into early retirement just before the Wall came down. With the collapse of the GDR, he retreated from his political life. He began to spend more time with Markus and Clara, sometimes in Berlin, but mainly at their dacha in the forest. He went there because much of the forest had been opened up after decades as a restricted, military zone. The place where he had spent those final, fearful days at the end of the war was available to him again.

Almost immediately after the forest was reopened to the general public, people started finding bodies in the woods. They were the remains of both soldiers and civilians, some of the tens of thousands who had died in those April weeks and who had been swallowed by the forest. An association was set up to find them, to give them a proper burial in a churchyard or military cemetery. Later, as they entered a new century, it was possible to use DNA to identify those that were found, but back in the 1990s it still seemed important to make sure they were found in the first place.

I asked Markus if his father went into the woods to search for his friend.

'At first I think he did,' he replied.

Klaus joined the association and began to help with the search. Over the years he found the remains of a number of victims of the last days and weeks of the war, but none that he thought were his friend. When they found the remains of a body in the woods, they had to call in the bomb squad in case of unexploded grenades. Then they would try and identify the person before, one way or the other, they were given a proper funeral. But Klaus always knew that none of the people found were his friend. If he had found him, he would have known it. But he never did. And he never found the farmhouse, where the beautiful woman had gathered her washing in the spring sunshine. But he was in his seventies then, and it was a long time after the events. Would he really remember? But, Markus continued, his father kept looking. He kept walking out from the dacha and into the woods, with his stick and, later, his metal detector, until he was unable to walk out there any more. Just before he died, the long search now over, he seemed at peace. It did not matter that he had not found his friend. At least he had tried.

'And,' Markus said, 'I'm sure he began to think that maybe he had given him a proper burial in the first place.' After all, neither of them were religious. Maybe it was right that he had left him in the forest. Maybe it was right that his friend was left, resting there, beneath the pine trees and a scrap of blue sky, where he fell.

On one occasion I was able to persuade K. that we should take Markus up on his offer of a visit to the dacha. We caught the train from Alexanderplatz, following the river where pleasure cruisers jostled for space, top decks filled with bald heads and beer glasses and the sound of competing commentaries telling the story of the city in a multitude of languages. From the train we looked out across scruffy wasteland spaces and through apartment windows for fleeting glimpses of interior lives. We passed office blocks and a power station, rail yards and cemeteries, and many messages, aimed at the world, sprayed on the walls.

1. FC UNION!
NO ISLAM!
ANTIFA!

PAUL SCRATON

Above allotment gardens, German flags and Ferrari banners hung limply from rusting poles. Construction workers laboured in the sunshine on new estates of detached houses. The city and the countryside mingled for a while beyond the train window. A field of horses and an expanse of forest. An industrial park and another new estate. For a moment the train stopped on a bridge, offering a view down the canal to a mooring of houseboats, and gardens running down to the water's edge.

The train dropped us in the closest village to where Markus and Clara had their dacha. Signs pointed the way to the campground and the lake, a two-kilometre walk away. We followed a paved road that turned to dirt before becoming a sandy track. Mosquitoes hassled us in the shade. When we arrived, Markus was watering his flowers. The swimming pool shimmered, as did the air above the barbecue that was already lit. Clara, he told us, had gone into the city for a doctor's appointment, so he was pleased we could make it. We left our bags in the garden and went down to the lake for a swim. When we returned, Markus handed us beers and we sat on the veranda, waiting for the sausages to cook. K. was quiet. Markus too. He only livened up when offering us something to eat or drink, or when he heard the call of a bird in the woods. He told us about the pygmy owls, and how there were only ten breeding pairs left in the area. He had never seen one, not in all the years they had been coming to the dacha, but he would love to. The forest continued to hide, continued to offer sanctuary.

It was why he loved it, he said, turning the meat on the grill. Because it is part of us, this forest. It contains our story. The good and the bad.

As the evening went on, it became clear that Markus was troubled. It was not Clara, he insisted. The appointment was rearranged, but otherwise routine. It was later, as we sat in the light of paraffin torches, that he told us what was bothering him. One of the young boys from the neighbouring house, which belonged to a new family from somewhere outside Leipzig, had made a comment when Markus greeted him across the garden fence. He didn't blame the boy. The child was only repeating, surely, something he had heard from his parents. But he did not like the idea of his past being used against him. Not here. Not in this place.

'I don't know why you are surprised.'

K. was sat back, out of the glow of the torches, lost to the darkness.

Markus was silent for a moment, and then he spoke.

'No, I don't suppose I should be. But I had always thought, in this place...'

Another pause.

He had always known what people thought of him and people like him, he continued. Those who had done the work he had done. And yet he had always slept easy in his bed. He knew what he had done and the reasons he had done it. The rest was rumour, conjecture. Nobody even asked! But he knew. Yes, he slept easy in his bed.

But the boy's remarks troubled him, K. insisted in the darkness, because deep down he must surely know that what had been done could not be justified. Not then, and not now.

Another pause.

'It was the same with Konrad,' Markus said, his voice soft, barely audible despite the silence of the dacha colony in the woods. It was after the Wall came down, he continued, when he had started meeting Konrad again. At Franz's pub, with Otto. Out there, at the dacha, when the three friends would walk together, by the lake. Konrad liked to quote Stefan Heym when the subject of the GDR came up. They had been living, Konrad said, using Heym's words, in a *land of crooked spines*. People were so used to looking over their shoulders, their backs were twisted. And Konrad would say it was a land of liars too, where everyone, even people like Markus – *especially* people like Markus – were all too scared to voice their thoughts, to let pass their lips what they truly felt. It made hypocrites of them all.

'Do you agree with him?'

'There was corruption,' he said. 'A corruption of values, of what we were supposed to be defending.'

He saw it in the Ministry. On the street and in the colony. Sometimes it was his job to expose it. Entries in a file, things that might become useful one day. But he had personally, he insisted, never done anything to benefit himself. Not once. He could sleep easy on that too. There was only one time, he continued, when he had used his power, or his influence, for anything other than the cause for which it had been granted. That was for Konrad. And although Markus saved him in that moment, he destroyed things between them. Their friendship was soured, tainted. Oh, later they would sit and drink together and Konrad would come out to the dacha, to sit on a camping chair just like we were doing that evening, but Markus could hear it in his voice, hear the disdain, the absence of love. After Otto died, Konrad stopped drinking in the pub. He never came to the dacha. In one moment, Markus had lost both his best friends. And he knew that a good part of it was because of what he had been, even if that was never all that he was.

He still believed that what his father saw being born out of the ruins of Berlin was worth fighting for, he continued, and I sensed he was talking as much to himself now as he was to us. Try to imagine what came before. When the stories from the camps came out, people pretended they hadn't known. But his father called that for the nonsense it was. *Of course we knew,* he said. Every child knew the jokes. The sad thing, Markus said, was that both he and Konrad learned the same lessons, the same ones his father taught. But their paths were different, and Konrad would never forgive Markus for the one that he took, the same one as his father. Should he apologise for that now? For not seeing any alternative? They bought into the system as it was, for all its flaws, because at that time they did not see another way.

'Maybe our methods were wrong,' he said, softly. 'Maybe we went about it all the wrong way. I can see that now, whatever others think. But what *was* the alternative?'

The question hung in the silence.

It was K. who spoke next.

'It was Konrad,' she replied. 'He was trying to show you, trying to tell you, all along.'

I did not see Markus again until the autumn, when I found him at his usual stool at the end of the bar, the tan from a long summer at the dacha still visible on his face. He called me over to join him, to offer me a drink. Our visit that evening, he said, had left him with a lot to think about. There was a time, in the 1980s, before the Wall came down and when everything seemed fixed for a hundred years or more, that he had begun to feel uneasy. He was only starting to understand this now. At the time he had blamed these growing feelings on tiredness, or overwork. He had started spending more and more time at the dacha. Every weekend in the summer months. Any day off. Clara was still working, and sometimes she had to be in the office on Saturdays, but he would go out there alone. It was a safe place, he said, despite those who owned the cabins around him. At the dacha, he did not need to deal with all the things that were making him increasingly uneasy, about the state and the system and his place in it. It was a place where he could forget, for a time, all of that and the everyday annoyances of life in the GDR that, even for someone in his position, had a certain impact on how he lived his life.

'The crooked spines,' he said.

Back then, in the GDR, he chose not to deal with it. He pushed the feelings of unease aside and ran away to the dacha. And later, when all their work and all their commitment was not only being dismissed but even criminalised, and the newspapers were printing names and addresses, photographs captured on a street corner, and the files were opened for all to see, then the dacha became a different type of sanctuary. He was running away still. So when the boy… Markus paused, as if the memory of what the boy had said to him was too painful to recall.

'I was scared,' he said, looking down at his glass. 'I was scared I would have to give it up.'

*

'Tough,' K. replied, when I told her what Markus had said, back at the apartment that evening. It was clear that she wanted to waste no more words on the subject.

VII

The Last Crofter

When Annika left Berlin she was pregnant, and by the time her daughter Isi arrived in the world, Annika and her boyfriend Adam were living in the small house overlooking the drained flood fields of the Oder River, a house that stood on raised ground with the polders and the Polish border to the east and a dense forest to the west. At the foot of their hill was a village, a collection of low houses along a single street that ran between Annika's hill and the old manor house, now a children's home, and the carp ponds with their elaborate netting to prevent poaching by passing ospreys and white-tailed eagles. The village was surrounded by the border landscape of the river and the dykes that controlled the flooding of the polders, forests and farmed fields, grazing meadows and marshlands. Annika's house sat above it all, in a small colony of mostly weekend cabins, some of which had been converted into permanent residences. Their house was small, with two bedrooms and a tiny kitchen on the ground floor, and a conservatory that looked out across the terraced gardens to the polders and the river beyond.

When they made their decision to leave Berlin, it had been Adam's dream to have a place where he could build his furniture. The basement of their house was a single room, lit by high windows and strip lights, that became not only Adam's workshop but also home to Annika's drawing table. When they set up the workshop, they imagined spending their days down there together, engaged in their projects, inspired by each other. Later, Annika would say that she could count on one hand the number of days it actually worked out like that. In the early months, she was busy with Isi and had no head for work. When Isi slept, Annika told herself she should go down there and sit at the drawing table, if only to remind herself of what else she was. But Annika was tired herself, and so when Isi slept, she slept, even if the vision of the blank white page floated before her as she drifted off.

It was around that time that the house, having given them half a year or so of grace, began to make demands of its own. A cracked window frame and a small leak in the guttering. Roof tiles blown down the terraced garden in a storm. And although the general costs of living out there on the edge were so much lower than in Berlin, they were still more than Adam could hope to pay through painstaking work crafting bookcases or tables down in the basement. He took a job in the nearest town, about seven kilometres away along the tree-lined avenue that was the only road in or out of the village, and there he worked on bookcases and tables designed by others. He was part of a team of five men who got on well together, enjoying the work and the company. It was steady and regular, not too taxing, and a few evenings a week he would stay in town after work for drinks with his colleagues, sending a message to Annika that if she was hungry, she did not need to wait for his return.

For the most part, in those early months, Annika was content. She spent hours with Isi in the conservatory, her view switching between the deep intensity of her gaze upon her daughter as she lay on the soft mat or dozed on Annika's lap, and the wide vista beyond the window as Annika charted the shift in the seasons, visible in the fields and the forest, the amount of smoke in the air and the nature of the light. In that first summer and autumn, Annika was appreciating the things that the city couldn't offer, and enjoying the absence of those that it could. When Annika called, she told us about the village, which she explored with Isi strapped to her front, the presence of a baby helping to break down the barriers of suspicion between long-established locals and the newcomers in their small house on the hill. She told us about the birds she had spotted from the conservatory and her first tentative explorations of the forest. She outlined plans for solar panels and a desire, formed in one of the few moments of the day she had for idle thought, to learn to ride a horse.

We did not see her much after she left Berlin. Once a month she would arrange a date to speak to K., and they would talk on the phone for an hour or so, the news reported to me later. Isi had started nursery. Adam had upped his hours at work. Annika had taken a job at the village bakery, three mornings a week. Some of the necessary changes were being made to the house. The reports from the edge of the country remained positive. Until they didn't.

BUILT ON SAND

*

K. took the phone call from Annika on a Wednesday evening. Could she come out to the house? It was not urgent, but Annika could use some company. Adam was away for a few days, she was alone with Isi, and she was feeling lonely. It wasn't urgent, she repeated, suggesting that it was.

When K. got to the house on Friday morning, Annika was in good spirits. Isi was at nursery and Annika had just come off a long phone call with Adam that seemed to have brightened her mood. She was sorry, she said as she busied herself making coffee in the small kitchen, if she had worried her friend, but at that particular moment she had felt an overwhelming urge to see her. K. told her she did not have to apologise and that she only ever had to ask. It was nice, K. continued, stepping out into the conservatory, to escape from the city for a while, whatever the reason.

After coffee they went out, following a steep path down the back of the hill until they reached the forest. Annika had lived there for almost two years by this point, and those first tentative explorations of the paths through the trees had been replaced with a proprietorial sense of belonging. As they walked, Annika talked about the different trees that they passed, about how pagans used to dedicate oaks to their gods, and how the Germans had continued this special relationship with oaks long after they'd converted to Christianity. She spoke of how this connection to the forest informed artists, from Dürer's woodcuts as he attempted to portray the sacred, to Goethe and Holderlin and the idea of the forest as a pure and spiritual holy wilderness. Inspired, Annika had been down to the workshop, using some of

103

PAUL SCRATON

Adam's offcuts from a long abandoned project to make her first experiments with woodcuts of her own. She wanted to use the forest to depict the forest, to reflect the sense of peace she felt as she moved along its mossy trails.

She was also reading fairy tales to Isi, and although they remained as gruesome as she remembered from her own childhood, she no longer thought of the forest as a place that was dark and sinister, but rather something pure, a place uncorrupted by the worst of what humans created in the clearings that they made. Everyone is equal in the woods, she said. The hunter or the elf, the woodcutter or the princess, the hermit or the highwayman. Hierarchy and class fell away among the trees. Nobody could own it, not really. Nobody could possess the forest, even if you had a piece of paper with your name on it. Those rules didn't apply.

They walked on, Annika pointing out the differences between the patches of older woodland and newer plantations with their severe, straight lines of red-brown pine trees. They spotted flashes of colour as jays crossed the path with a squawking call. They heard woodpeckers and saw families of deer, and the turned-over ground where wild boar had scavenged and dug at the black soil. There was a photographer Annika liked who took his pictures of the forest by waiting for hours for that moment just after a rain shower and which lasted only a couple of minutes, when the light was just right. She had never met him, but she could see him sitting there, in a tent or makeshift shelter, the rain hammering down above his head, waiting and waiting and waiting for the perfect moment.

They reached the edge of the woods, where a bench had been placed for hikers to stop and look out over the fields that stretched away to the north. In the distance, wind turbines turned above brown, ploughed fields. Smoke rose from a farmhouse chimney. The air had that first hint of coldness that told them autumn had arrived.

There was a house, Annika said, on the edge of the woods, not far from where they sat. It was a stone building with a new roof, surrounded by high fences. She had discovered the house during one of her earliest walks in the woods, and back then it was completely shuttered up, with padlocks on the doors and a garden of overgrown brambles, ferns and saplings. To Annika it seemed almost perfect, tucked away on the edge of the woods down a forester's track, surrounded by the trees.

At work she began to ask around, questioning those who had lived in the village for years or even decades. They did not seem to know much about what could be found in the forest. Some of her colleagues had never been deep into the woods, including one whose garden backed onto the first of the trees. She only ever went in there to retrieve her son's football when it sailed over the fence. But even if people had never seen the house in the forest, they had heard the stories. In the GDR it was used by the local authorities. Some said it was for the foresters to store their equipment, others that it had been a place for the border guards patrolling the area to take a break. In the 1990s it was sold off, bought by a man who arrived in the village driving an Audi. The different versions of the story Annika heard agreed on the make of car, but not the origins of the driver. Some said he was German, from the West. Others that he was Swedish, Bulgarian or Greek. The car had number plates registered to Berlin. Or Halle. Or Frankfurt-an-der-Oder. The new owner installed fortified windows and new doors, and a high fence around the property. No one saw the man with the Audi again, but they heard plenty about what was supposedly going on there. Cigarettes from Poland. Drugs from Lebanon. Girls from the Balkans.

But that had been then, Annika said, and all agreed that things had been quiet since the turn of the century. Slowly, she forgot about the house. It wasn't on the route of any of her regular walks through the forest, and as she stopped asking, people stopped telling her the stories. But a few months later, there was a new tale to be told in the bakery queue. Someone was living in the house. Each time she heard of the new forest dweller, things became more fantastical. A refugee who had sneaked across the river. A criminal on the run. For a few days, the story was that he was a convicted paedophile, recently released from prison. There were whispers that he was from a cult and had brought black magic into the woods, like the pagans with their oak trees. And yet, nobody had seen him, and he had never been into the village. It was all second-hand.

For Annika, standing behind the bakery counter, she could feel the malignancy of the gossip, of which this story was just one of many. It ate away at the people and the community, fuelling fears and resentments, and yet everyone was a part of it. The more outrageous, the more impossible the story, the better it seemed to be and the more hurriedly it was passed on. At the same time, there were factual stories about the village that no one ever spoke about. At the library, Annika discovered there had been an outpost of the Ravensbrück concentration camp in the village, a satellite camp for forced labourers, working the fields and quarries. When they died, they were buried on the edge of the village in unmarked graves. They were still there, the graves, and yet no one was interested. Instead, they spoke of who was fucking who, and a refugee paedophile supposedly living in the woods, who nobody had even seen and yet who, like the returning wolves, was biding his time, waiting to target the children innocently playing football in their gardens...

Annika fell silent. K. could see her eyes were wet.

K. asked her what the matter was, but Annika shook her head and stood up. It was nearly time to pick up Isi from nursery. They walked back to the house in silence, Annika lost in thought and a step or two ahead as they moved down the path. It was only later, after Isi's bedtime, that Annika returned to her story and the house on the edge of the woods.

She had decided to go and look for herself. Having dropped Isi off one morning, she walked through the village and across the stream that marked the boundary between the last of the houses on the road towards town and the start of the woods. Hiking trails were marked here, with green arrows pointing in different directions, their distances and destinations painted in neat, white letters and numbers. The quickest route to the house was along an unmarked trail, which existed on no maps and was part of no hiking route. Annika made her way swiftly through the trees, only slowing as the house began to appear in the distance.

The heavy door was open. The glass had been cleaned and there was smoke coming from the chimney. The high fence remained, but it too was open, offering an uninterrupted view across the once overgrown garden, which was now cleared. There she could see a man working the ground, turning over a mix of soil and plant remains, as a pile of cuttings and twigs burned in the corner. As she approached, the man turned and greeted her with a smile. His name was Hannes. They talked at the gate for a while, introducing themselves. He was from Berlin, he said, although not originally. He had rented the house from a friend of a friend. There was, Annika remembered thinking at the time, the suggestion of a deeper story, of a loss or some other trauma that had led him to this house in the woods, but they were still strangers then. He invited her in for a cup of coffee. As they drank, Hannes told her about his plans for the house. A vegetable patch and a chicken run. Maybe even a pig. He had heard about the return of the wolves to that part of the forest, but he wasn't worried. He had the high fence.

'He made me laugh,' Annika said. After that first visit, she returned to the house at least two or three times a week. She would sit on an upturned log that Hannes had fashioned into a stool and watch him while he worked on the garden. They would talk for hours at a time, but never about the past. Instead, they spoke of his plans for the house and about her artwork. He questioned her gently about why it was she wasn't facing the white blank page. One day, after she told him about her experiments with woodcuts, he went into town on his motorbike and returned with a book from the library, about sculpture made from found objects in the forest. He thought it might interest her. The next morning, she went down to the basement for the first time in weeks and began to sketch some ideas.

K. tried to find out if they had been lovers, but Annika

refused to give a clear answer. Ultimately, it didn't matter. Emotionally they had been, K. was convinced of that, which was more important than the details of the what, where, when and how. Instead, Annika told her about their conversations, about Goethe and Dürer and Holderlin, about jays and woodpeckers and wild boar, about the forest and the world beyond. She asked Hannes why he never went to the village, and he told her he had moved to the house to escape people, not to be the centre of attention. To really escape, he said, you either had to disappear among people, in a big city where no one knows you, or you had to go to a place where there really was no one to bother you. In a small village like that one, it was impossible to hide.

K. asked her about Adam, about what he knew about Hannes, about the house in the woods, the mornings Annika had spent there, and what it was that had inspired her back to the drawing board in the basement.

Nothing, Annika replied. She had told him nothing, and now it didn't matter, because Hannes had gone. He had disappeared, and so what was there left to tell?

The next morning, Annika loaded Isi into her pushchair and walked with K. down the hill to the dyke, and the path that ran across the polder towards the river and the border with Poland. As the path dropped down, Annika spoke of the strange feeling it gave her as she followed this low path between the two dykes, to know that they were walking below both the river and the canal and that, should either of the dykes fail, the water would rush in and soon be above their heads. When the marshes were drained and the dykes built to create the dry polders, the land was settled by people from other flat lands far away. From the border with the Netherlands and up by Denmark, places where people were familiar with reclaimed land and knew how to farm it. This was two hundred years before, and yet there was still a divide between the 'old' villages that had been built on raised patches of land above the marshes and the 'new' sister villages of the settlers. The rivalries between the sibling communities continued two centuries on, between the original marsh dwellers and the colonists, where the scandal of mixed marriages and the idea of moving from one side to the other remained.

Across the polder, they climbed the opposite embankment to the dyke that ran alongside the river. On each bank, painted poles marked the border. In Germany, cyclists travelled north in a stretched-out line. In Poland, a fisherman waded in the shallows.

About a year before she had moved to the village, Annika said as they looked downstream, a girl had gone missing, almost exactly at the spot where they now stood. The girl was sixteen, and when the search party reached the riverside path, they found her shoes and clothes, neatly folded by the water's edge. Her phone was there, and a towel. It was presumed she had gone swimming and got into difficulty. It seemed likely that she had been swept away by the currents, but her body was never found. The gossips in the bakery queue, after waiting for a few days, began to whisper of problems at home. Maybe she had swum out with no intention of swimming back. But Annika liked to think she had found a way to disappear. Sick of waiting for the dykes to fail and wash it all away, she had left a false set of clues by the side of the river and simply ridden off to start again somewhere else. In Poland or Hamburg. Berlin or London.

Annika wondered if it was truly possible to disappear, with the internet and social media, facial recognition software and communication channels that effortlessly crossed borders and boundaries. She spoke about those people who had come into her life and gone away again, not to be found however much she searched. Of course, unless they had died without her knowing, they hadn't disappeared to the people who remained in their lives. They had just disappeared to her.

Annika pulled out her phone. Sometimes she opened her email account and expected to see a message from Hannes. But one never arrived.

She sat down on the grassy slope beneath the path. Isi slept in the pushchair. They watched the river moving past. It had a deceptive speed. You would think you could swim and would only discover you didn't have the strength to make it across or back when it was too late.

Annika had made a decision. She had gone to Hannes to tell him what it was. First Hannes, then Adam. As she walked along the path to the house, she felt lighter than she had done for years. She had with her the book that he had brought her from the library, and one of her sketches. She was so lost in her thoughts that she did not see the woman until she was almost upon her. Their coming together made Annika jump, surprised not only because she had not seen the woman approaching, but because she had never met anyone on that stretch of path, so close to Hannes's house. The woman was friendly, smiling an apology. She was walking in the opposite direction from Annika, away from the house. She was carrying a basket for mushrooms and Annika could remember her black boots and white dress, and a red leather jacket.

Annika had hurried on, a sense of urgency suddenly overwhelming her, needing to tell Hannes her decision, to make it real before her courage failed. In her memory she was running the last few hundred metres, the trees and forest floor a blur, as if it had all been turned over by a hungry wild boar. But when she got to the house it was all locked up. The gate and the door. The windows were covered. The garden was overgrown. How long had it been since she was last there? Surely it had been less than a week? Could the forest have reclaimed a garden in such a short period of time? Could it really have erased all trace? She walked the perimeter, peering in through the fence, trying to find a clue, trying to see some trace of Hannes. A scrap of litter. A burned patch from a bonfire. But there was nothing there.

As she walked home, she felt the heaviness return. She reached the house an hour before it was time to go pick up Isi. Adam was already there, waiting in the conservatory. She had forgotten she'd asked him to come home early. Forgotten that she had made plans to tell him the news. He had been worried, he said, as she stood in the doorway. What was it she wanted to talk about? It was nothing important, she replied. She just thought that maybe the solar panels could wait. Maybe they could take a trip for a few weeks. They could go on a small holiday. The three of them. It would be good for them, she said, feeling empty inside.

Online, she searched for information about the cabin, finding a listing on a real estate website. The next morning, she called the number. The woman at the other end was surprised to hear Annika call, as that property had been listed for years but with very little interest. No one had even looked at it, the woman said, once she had found the right folder on her computer, not since it had been determined by the council that the property could not be used as a residence, not even as a weekend house for overnight stays. She began to explain to Annika how this limited the potential market and how she had told the owner he would have to lower the price, but Annika was not really listening. Politely, she declined the offer to go and have a look at the house and hung up the phone.

On the riverbank, Annika lay back and looked up at the sky. Sometimes, she said, when Adam was at his worst, she imagined taking him into the forest and leaving him there. It was possible, she thought, to get lost in the forest.

Across the river, a kestrel hovered above a Polish field, in search of a meal.

K. waited, as Annika closed her eyes.

'I can't explain it,' Annika said. Nothing made sense to her. Ever since Hannes left there had been no mention of him in the bakery queue. All the whispers and the stories, all the theories and the fears that had been passed around the village from the moment he arrived, had stopped. They had vanished without trace, just like he had. Maybe, she said, sitting up as Isi stirred in her pushchair, it really was possible to disappear. The two friends looked across the river from where they sat, scanning an empty sky on both sides of the border. Above the Polish field there was no longer any sign of the kestrel that had been hanging there, above the wheat, only moments before.

VIII

Heimat

After living in Berlin for about a year, working towards her doctorate, Charlotte returned to Canada for the summer. She stayed with her parents, in the Toronto suburbs, and experienced that uneasy feeling of 'returning' to a home that she had never lived in. Much of the furniture was the same as in her childhood home, and many of the pictures on the wall. It still smelled of the chosen brand of washing powder and her father's vanilla-scented cigarillos, but the beds and bookshelves were now standing in different rooms and the same rugs had been laid on different floors. All the views from the windows were new to her, and on the first evening she got up from the dinner table and was halfway to the door before realising she needed to ask where the bathroom was. It made her miss the sense of security she had developed in her Berlin apartment, despite spending the previous twelve months trying to understand how the city of her father's birth actually worked.

On the night before she flew back to Berlin, her father handed her a folder. The last of the shipments of boxes from her grandparents' house in Germany had finally arrived in Canada. Although Charlotte had been there as her father sorted through the house with its decades of accumulated personal belongings, there had been whole boxes of photographs, papers and other effects that he had felt unable to deal with at the time, and he'd had them shipped to Toronto, including the folder he handed to his daughter on the final evening. It was a collection of photographs, old postcards and a couple of diaries that had belonged to his mother, her grandmother, dating back to her late teenage years when she was a young woman, preparing to leave her childhood home, the city she called Danzig.

Charlotte's grandmother was named Alice, and at the end of the Second World War, Alice and her family travelled west on a refugee train, moving only with what they could carry by hand, from a city that no longer wanted them to a place they had no connection to at all. Some of their belongings had to be jettisoned en route, when the train stopped short of what was now the Polish-German border, and they were told they had to walk alongside four kilometres of badly damaged track until they reached another train. Alice did not care for her clothes or, indeed, most of what was in her suitcase. Not really. But she kept her small cardboard folder close, packed with just her most important pictures and memories of a place that she sensed, even in those last moments among the rubble of the badly damaged city, she might never see again. The city of her childhood and adolescence. Of peacetime and war. Of family love and first kisses. The Danzig that was also Gdańsk, on the banks of the Mottlau River that was also the

Motława. In her diary, on her last morning before they took the train, she wrote that even if she had to say goodbye to her home city, at least she could take something of it with her.

At the end of the war, Alice was seventeen. The diary that she wrote during the final months in Danzig and the first few weeks in Berlin was the only one she ever kept. It detailed the events of everyday life in a city where they knew the end was coming. It could hardly get any worse. Much of the city centre was destroyed, with whole rows of buildings wiped out, leaving behind only the front steps that led up, not to a door with a heavy brass knocker, but a pile of rubble and an empty space. Alice wrote in German, with odd words and phrases in both Polish and Kashubian because, like so many families in Danzig/Gdańsk, hers was a mix. In some entries she wrote of how she wished they could have been left alone, describing the German administrators and soldiers as an occupying army. Elsewhere she scribbled, hurriedly, on an otherwise empty page, that *it looks as if we are going to lose the war.*

Germany as 'they'.

Germany as 'we'.

To Charlotte, as she first looked over the collection of photographs and postcards Alice had taken with her to Berlin, it was clear that her grandmother was taking with her the memories of a place that was both hers and which had already been destroyed. The postcards were of buildings, or images of the harbour and views of the Main Town skyline from across the river. These were the landmarks of the city, some of which would later be rebuilt as if nothing had happened and some of which would exist only in the recollections of those who had experienced them, for as long as they might live. The photographs were mainly of people. Of Alice's family and friends, their names scribbled in pencil on the back. She had gathered them all together and held them close on her journey to Berlin, and they arrived safely in a city that, almost unimaginably, seemed to be in a greater level of devastation and despair than the one she had left behind.

In Berlin, she met a fellow refugee; the Baltic teenager finding the Silesian farmer among the crowds of dispossessed. A couple of years later she was pregnant and married. That was the moment Alice cut her ties to the past, making a decision to finally leave Danzig behind her. Her son could remember a neighbour once asking her where she was originally from, as they made small talk over the back fence of their Berlin garden. It didn't matter, Alice told the neighbour. She had forgotten all about it. For Alice, who had both a young child to deal with and a husband who spent his days in mourning for his own lost homeland as he turned his once-pleasant soul bitter and twisted, it was more important to live in the *here* of the present and not in the *there* of memory.

And yet: for all those years she kept the folder and her diary, her photographs and postcards; a tiny sliver of Danzig and the youthful Alice which remained hidden in the boxes in the attic as she moved through life, and long after she died.

When Charlotte read the diary, sitting in the window seat of a plane high over the North Atlantic, she could sense Alice's love for the place she knew she was about to leave behind. She could sense her grandmother's rootedness, to those streets and the surrounding countryside, as she used all three languages of her heritage and made notes of memories she was not yet willing to surrender, of people and places, and recipes she would cook in her Berlin kitchen. She loved her city as much as she hated the people with their flags

and songs who had destroyed it, who had forced them all
to choose which side they were on and brought catastrophe
down upon all their heads. When Charlotte arrived back in
Berlin, she called her father to tell him she'd arrived safely
and to ask him about Alice. Had she ever been back to
Gdańsk? Her father told her no, she hadn't, and neither had
he. Even after the Wall came down, when a visit to the city of
Alice's childhood would have meant a straightforward six-
hour train ride, she showed no interest in returning. However
well they might have rebuilt the city, recreating the Danzig /
Gdańsk from before the bombs fell, she knew it wouldn't be
the same. Charlotte wondered if she had ever looked at her
photographs or read her diary, as an older woman, returning
to the city in her memory even as she declined a visit in
reality. Unlike her husband, who returned time and again in
his head to the Silesia of before the war, if anything Alice
spoke even less about her childhood and her Baltic home
as she got older. But then, as Charlotte's father said to his
daughter down the phone line, she was at peace with her
past by the end, whereas Charlotte's grandfather never was.

I met Charlotte in a cafe, not long after she returned from a
trip to Gdańsk. She had made the decision to travel to the
Baltic city soon after her visit to Canada. She had gone there
not so much in search of her grandmother's story, but to fill
in some of the gaps. Even if most of it had been destroyed
and then rebuilt, she thought, it must be possible to get a
sense of how it would have been experienced by Alice as a
young woman.

The cafe where I met Charlotte was on a street that, in the years of Alice's Danzig childhood, was in a working-class district of Berlin full of street hawkers and newspaper vendors, basement bars and backroom brothels; a neighbourhood of courtyards where untidy children roamed, and where Döblin and Roth stalked the streets in search of stories as bands of Nazis and Communists spoiled for a fight. By the time I met Charlotte, almost a century later, the street had been through many shifts, from wartime devastation to socialist hibernation in the GDR, underground bars and squatted tenement blocks in the 1990s, to a twenty-first-century homeland for the citizens of nowhere, a *heimat for the cosmopolitans*, as one German weekly newspaper put it. It was a street lined with bare-brick-walled coffee shops, oxymoronic street food restaurants and international fashion brands. The GDR residents, the underground bar dwellers and the squatters were long gone, and the old tenement blocks had been renovated, one by one.

The cafe was pleasant enough, with its brick walls and wooden floors, a coffee machine that cost more than some of the cars parked outside and tasteful photographs of the old city as it once existed beyond the front door, back when the neighbourhood was fed on a diet of pea soup and sausages, the air heavy with exhaust fumes and brown coal smog, and clouds of Russian tobacco. That was a memory now, for anyone returning to see how the neighbourhood had changed. Inside the cafe, it didn't really matter. Photographs aside, it could have been anywhere.

'I went to a place like this each morning in Gdańsk,' Charlotte said as she ordered a tea. It was in an old printworks, but otherwise it felt just like the cafe in Berlin, or those she had been to in Toronto or London, Stockholm or Barcelona. She shrugged at what this said about her. At least the coffee was usually good.

She travelled to Gdańsk on the late train, crossing the bridge into Poland about an hour after departure. It was late summer and still light as the train moved across a landscape of sun-scorched fields and dense forests, travelling ever northwards to the Baltic with an assorted cast of changing characters, until it reached the end of the line. She arrived after dark, but the air was still warm and the streets were thronged with people, in the parks and cafe terraces, outside the pubs and down on the harbour.

She felt comfortable from the first moment, settling into a room close to the harbour in a flat shared by a group of Polish students, who rented the spare room to travellers to make some extra beer money. They took her out on that first night, giving her time only to drop her bags before they began a whirlwind tour of late cafes and basement bars, of beer and vodka and watching the sun come up over the rebuilt Main Town. They had asked her politely what it was she was in town to do, but showed little interest in her answer. They had their own concerns, with their studies and their love lives, the direction of their country and their government. One of Charlotte's hosts was thinking of leaving for London. All politicians were bad, he said, as they sat at sunrise with their legs dangling over the quayside, but they were easier to ignore when they were not your own.

That first morning, Charlotte slept for a few hours before dragging herself back out onto sunny streets as lunchtime approached. She had found an old map of the city online, and comparing that with a contemporary street plan and the names of places written in Alice's diary she was able to plot a course through the Main Town and the Old Town as well as out, past the station, to the outlying districts. On the map she marked the landmarks of a childhood: the apartment and the school, the church and the location of a Saturday job, the home of an aunt, close to where Günter Grass grew up, and the post office where a dramatic siege marked the early days of a long, long war.

'That first morning,' she said to me in Berlin, 'I understood something that I already knew but that I hadn't quite grasped: there was very little left.'

Under an arched gateway in the Main Town she found a photograph, an image of the city taken from above in the days around the time that Alice was packing her bag to start out on the journey to Berlin. It showed the vast majority of the city centre levelled. Charlotte could see in the photograph those staircases Alice had written about in her diary, the ones that led up from the pavement to piles of rubble and the fragile skeleton frames of gutted houses. Close to the station, it was possible for Charlotte to read this destruction in the streets themselves, in the post-war housing blocks and communist-era hotels and more modern structures, from shopping centres to new office towers. But in the Main Town, Gdańsk had been replicated, as if back in its Hanseatic heyday. If Alice had been able to walk with Charlotte along Długi Targ, the long, main square, she would have recognised much of it. But it was almost all just a facade, and behind the elegant frontages of coloured tiles and crow-stepped gables were concrete blocks built to the same plan as countless others from Berlin to Vladivostok, and all the places in between.

The reimagination of old Danzig / Gdańsk was impressive, but not quite complete. On one street in the Main Town, Charlotte found a row of staircases where the empty spaces behind them had simply been left. These were front steps that led up to nothing. The more Charlotte looked, the more she discovered traces of her grandmother's city. Around the back of the station she came to a walled garden, set back from the road. In the years after the German-speaking population had been removed from Gdańsk, many graves had been cleared away, as if in a conscious attempt to pretend that the city had never been home to a multitude of languages, religions and other cultural groups. There was, it seemed, no desire for the dead to remind the living of the city as it had once been. In the early years of the twenty-first century, an art project was commissioned to create what Charlotte had stumbled upon, the Cemetery of Lost Cemeteries, where fragments of those bulldozed headstones from across the city had been brought together to create a memorial to those who had once called the city home. Charlotte walked up and down the rows as the traffic streamed by on the road outside the gates, and workmen fixed the roof of a neighbouring church to the sound of pop music and hyperactive radio advertisements. The headstones were damaged, with pieces missing. Some were in German, others in Hebrew. Some offered full names, others only a part. Charlotte wondered if her ancestors were represented there. She knew no names, other than her grandmother's maiden name, but in the end it didn't matter whether she could identify a family member on the fragments of headstones or not. Of course they were represented there. That was the whole point.

She was chasing ghosts, but as the days passed by, she also discovered the other city. The place of Lech Walesa and the shipyards, of European Football Championships and contemporary debates about how history should be told. Her temporary flatmates helped her grasp their own Gdańsk in between her explorations of Alice's Danzig. At the end of her short visit, she knew she had to go back. There hadn't been enough time. On the train back to Berlin, she wondered what her grandmother must have thought, watching the evening news in West Berlin in the early 1980s as her home city became the centre of the world's attention. Did she see in those images the city of her birth and childhood, or had it become by then simply someplace else, just another foreign city behind the Iron Curtain, like Budapest or Prague or even East Berlin, only a few kilometres away.

It was the problem with delving into the past, Charlotte said, as we finished our drinks and she prepared to leave. She had come back from Gdańsk with more questions, and there was no one to ask. Some would never be answered. Like the very idea of the Cemetery of Lost Cemeteries, the thought was bittersweet.

All cities shift. After she had gone, I pulled a newspaper out of my bag and ordered another coffee. It had been a hot summer, perhaps the hottest since my arrival in Berlin, and the city was uneasy. The pattern repeated itself on a weekly cycle. The heat would build, day by day. The tarmac grew sticky as the smell of slow-cooked sewage rose up from the drains on every corner. It would build until it felt like you could no longer breathe, and then it was released in a sudden, violent electrical storm, the water pouring from overwhelmed drainpipes and down the stairs of U-Bahn stations, lifting cars from where they were parked under bridges and tunnels, and flooding basements with their water-soaked boxes of old paperbacks and photo albums, turning all those stories into a slushy pulp.

It was a summer of unrest. Earlier in the year, the authorities had begun the process of clearing some of the last of the squatted houses in the centre of the city, places still holding on behind their crumbling facades and defiant slogans painted on the banners that hung from windowsills. There were not many left, but their removal was a symbol of the continuing shifts that had long been taking place. The action played out each time as if choreographed. The police arriving in force, their vans blocking off streets. Protestors arriving not long after, also in numbers. There were scuffles as the few remaining residents were led out from the building. Someone would inevitably end up on the roof, waving a flag. And then it would be over. The work crews would toil through the night to make the building secure and uninhabitable, and another Berlin story would come to an end. What it meant for the city would be debated in the pages of the press and online, on social media and blogs, as part of discussions about the steady increase in rents, the outside investment in real estate and the next version of Berlin that was taking shape before the eyes of all who lived here.

On that afternoon, in the cafe that stood in what was once the heart of Berlin's most desperate slum, the newspaper headlines could have come from any moment during my time in the city. Fortified borders and missile strikes. A refugee crisis and a potential peace deal. Tentative agreements and a tense, nil–nil draw. In Bavaria, Bayern Munich were champions. In Berlin, cars were burning by night, a parade of parked Audis, BMWs and Mercedes in Friedrichshain, Mitte and Kreuzberg, going up in flames as a symbolic or moronic representation, depending on your point of view, of the depth of feeling when it came to the changes taking place in the city.

One thing this writer cannot help but notice, is that of all the cars burned in Berlin over the past weekend, every single one of them was built by a German manufacturer... At the same time, if people are parking such cars along these streets that had once been the very front line of Berlin's resistance to the Liberal-Capitalist project, then perhaps the battle has already been lost...

It wasn't only cars. Brand new apartment blocks were peppered with paint-bombs the moment the scaffolding was removed. On a street in Mitte, an entire row of shops had their windows broken one Sunday evening. A developer of luxury lofts in an old factory complex sought to reassure potential purchasers by installing a car elevator, that would allow them to take their Mercedes, their BMW or their Audi up to their apartment with them. The city shifted once more.

Charlotte left the cafe having told me she was already planning a return to Gdańsk, even though she knew she could not find all the answers she was looking for. She questioned herself constantly about why she was doing this now. What did her grandmother's memories of Danzig matter anymore, now she was long dead? As she stood by the table, her bag already over her shoulder, she answered her own question. It mattered in the same way the destruction of an old building mattered, even if it was crumbling and no longer used for the purpose for which it was built. It mattered in the same way as the destruction of an old oak tree, hit by lightning in a storm. It was the connection to the past that mattered, otherwise what was left? It was precisely the fact that Alice was no longer around, that Charlotte had never had the chance to ask her those questions, that made her want to return to the city. Even if she could not fill in the gaps. Even if she ultimately knew that the steps from the street would always lead up to an empty space.

IX

Under the Sun

It was on the hottest of Berlin's summer days, when the heat seemed to heighten the sounds and smells of the city, that I would be taken back to the June day during my second year in Berlin when Tomas died. I had thought about that day so many times in the years that followed, that on those days when the temperature pushed past thirty-five and the roads grew soft it only took the smallest of triggers to return me there, to take me back into a moment or a scene, the actions playing out as they always had done, as I felt the sadness of knowing how it was all going to end. I would stand on the street corner or in the park, letting the sirens fade or the song finish on the radio, waiting for the moment to pass, waiting to return to the present, where Tomas is long gone and isn't ever coming back.

✳

On that June morning, we were sat in the kitchen when the doorbell rang. Tomas answered the intercom in the hall and buzzed the visitor up, opening the apartment door as he did so. He was back at his seat in the kitchen when K. appeared in the doorway, breathless from the bike ride and the stairs. She was there for Tomas, to join him on the demonstration that he had been planning for weeks. She was there for Tomas but it was me she looked to first, with a smile that reassured all the doubts that had been building in me. A few weeks earlier, K. had been Tomas's classmate, someone I had heard about more than I had seen. We had met in groups in a bar or at the park, had exchanged a few words, but it was nothing more than that. Not until the party, held in the apartment of someone long forgotten, in the deep south of the city, where we spent a long evening on the balcony together to escape the heat. She left first for the long journey home and kissed me, half on the lips. A few days later she called, inviting me to watch a film. I didn't know what to expect when I went to the cinema to meet her, and I was surprised and pleased to find that I was meeting her alone. That night we went back to her apartment together. Another kiss. This time the meaning was clearer, but I did not stay the night, even though I thought and hoped that we both wanted me to.

'What's with the two of you?' Tomas asked, the night before the demo, and I told him I didn't know. As she smiled in the kitchen doorway the next morning I had a better sense of things. I could read it in her face, in how she looked at me. There was something there.

The night before, I'd met Tomas in town after his final meeting, leaving the apartment with Boris as he loaded the last of his camping equipment into his Skoda. He had no interest in the demo, no interest in what had been building for weeks, in the press and on the internet. As the encampments of protestors from across the country and beyond set up in parks and playing fields across the city, Boris was driving north to a campsite by a lake, escaping the city before the road closures that threatened to shut down everything within the inner S-Bahn ring came into effect. I rode my bike to meet Tomas, two-lane roads all to myself, as the absence of parked cars and any real traffic gave the city an eerie feeling. When I met Tomas, he was receiving news of a skirmish in one of the parks only a couple of streets away and we went over to see, meeting lines of police blocking any access to the park as a helicopter hovered low above the treetops. It was one of the longest days of the year, but still the beam from the spotlight raked over the crowds, like a scene from a film as it cast huge shadows of the police line on the trees and buildings beyond.

Like the protestors, the police had been bussed in from across the country, and as Tomas made coffee in the kitchen that morning we watched as they moved in columns down our street. At the front were the vans, with their blue lights flashing but no sirens to be heard. Then came the police on foot, marching in line, eight across. Helmets hung loosely from their hips, covering their batons and guns. They were men and women, no doubt of different sizes and shapes, but from above only their hair colour and length distinguished them. As a mass, they looked oversized, solid and stuffed. Men and women. It didn't matter.

The low growl of the engines moving the vehicles at walking speed and the rhythmic thud of the heavy police boots on tarmac drifted ominously through the open kitchen window. Taking up the entire road, they drew residents to their windows, sending a message to the city as they moved beneath walls still pockmarked with bullet holes and shrapnel scars. K. and I stood at the window and watched them go by. Tomas leaned against the kitchen counter and watched us. He wasn't about to be intimidated.

Over coffee, we discussed the day. Tomas would be up front, on one of the trucks they had rented to carry the loudspeakers and the sound system. K. and I decided we would hang back, so we could tell Tomas later how the atmosphere had been elsewhere in the demo. They were expecting hundreds of thousands on the streets. Maybe even a million. More than Love Parade and New Year's Eve, Tomas said with a grin. What a message. Afterwards we were to meet at a beer garden, in the north and outside the restricted zone which would remain in place until the following morning. That was our rendezvous point. For drinks and a debrief; to celebrate the success of mobilising so many onto Berlin's streets. I remember Tomas was confident that it would stay peaceful, despite the ratcheting-up of tension in the press and the skirmishes the night before, despite the spate of car burnings and the rumoured arrival in town of thousands of the black bloc.

'It's going to be fine,' he said, when K. told him to stay safe as he left the apartment. He was going ahead for the marshals' meeting, to go over any last-minute changes to the plans. K. and I would follow later. He told us it was going to be fine and then let himself out of the apartment. We heard his footsteps on the staircase and the bang of the main house door crashing shut. It was going to be fine. Those were the last words we ever heard him speak.

By early afternoon we were in the middle of the procession, passing through the city centre and the landmarks of Berlin which appeared beyond the forest of banners and flags that surrounded us. The sun was high, right above the road, giving no chance of shade. Later, I would try and remember the order in which I had seen certain things as I tried to piece together the fragments of the day. The papier-mâché dolls of politicians, German and American, some of whom were in the city as we walked. The man, topless except for a high-vis jacket, selling beers from a cool box he had strapped to a shopping trolley. Another man, in a headband and with knee-high socks who looked like he was on his way to a roller disco. The woman with a wide-brimmed purple hat, who we followed for kilometre after kilometre. In my memory, there were lots of stewards but not many police. I asked K. where she thought they were, and she told me they were close by, there was no question about that. As the crowd thickened, we were pushed together. Bare arm against bare arm. She took my hand, so that we would not get separated. It got tighter, and, the pace of the procession slowed even more. Finally, we stopped.

Karl-Marx-Allee, between the tall palaces for the people, built to show how things had changed in the new Germany that was emerging from the wreckage of war. But we were not hemmed in by these grand apartment buildings, with their Meissen tiles that even from the beginning had fallen and threatened the heads of those on the wide pavements below. There were twelve lanes between the apartment blocks and plenty of open space. The street had been built big and wide to support military processions beneath scarlet banners. Build it big and make them feel small. And small we felt, under the beating sun. No, it was not the buildings, the people's palaces, that cut us off and brought us to a halt. It was the massed ranks of police, who had appeared now and were blocking us down the sides and, as the whispers passed up and down the crowd, at the front and the back as well. At first those around us in the crowd remained good-natured. Jokes about Berlin traffic and how we would have to hurry up soon because otherwise we were going to be late. Teasing chants aimed at anyone and everyone, and borrowed football songs, imported from the terraces to be heard on the grand, socialist boulevard. But as ten minutes became twenty, and then thirty became forty, the crowds were hushed. No more shouts now, no more music. Later, I remembered the sound of low conversations between friends, the buzz of a helicopter and sirens in the distance. K. sat down on the hot tarmac. Others did the same. On the edge of the crowds the police stood, impassive. Their helmets on. Visors down.

To pass the time, K. told me a story about the zoo. During the war, there were rumours after every bombing raid that the animals had escaped. There were crocodiles in the Spree and lions roaming the Ku'damm. Bears had laid claim to the Tiergarten while penguins swam the canals. It was either because the bombs had scored a direct hit on the enclosure walls, or because the never-ending scream of the falling bombs had caused the elephants to lose their minds and punch big holes in the wall. The story was that a lonely tiger would join the writers at the nearby cafe counter and the writers, K. said, would welcome him there because they were too drunk to notice, their inner emigration from the horrors of the regime fuelled by whatever alcohol the war-torn city could provide, distilled in bathtubs and brewed in the corners of basement bomb shelters. It was only later, when they realised the tiger had eaten all the cake, that the writers truly lost their minds, as outside the giraffes nibbled at the leaves of the only trees in the city that hadn't been felled for firewood.

On Karl-Marx-Allee, we were the ones enclosed, and with no elephants to clear us a pathway. From the balconies of apartment blocks, residents looked down on us; a colourful mass surrounded by black. The helicopter was closer now, dark against the brilliant blue sky. K. had finished her story and no one else was talking. Pings of text messages arriving sounded around us. It was not normal, K. said, standing up and urging me to do the same. Something was not right. It was not normal, she said again, only moments before the first whistle sounded.

Did it really start with a whistle? That was how I remembered it later. The sudden crackle of a thousand police radios and the sound of a single whistle. It was at that moment, as people scrambled to move whilst simultaneously realising there was nowhere they could move to, that I saw a column of black smoke rising in the distance. I guessed it was close to Alexanderplatz. After the whistle, an increase in pressure as a voice sounded over loudspeakers, instructing us to disperse. But there was still no direction in which we could go. If anything, at that moment, the crowd got tighter still as thousands of people instinctively huddled together for protection.

It was not normal.

And then: missiles overhead. Bottles and cans and broken sticks from placards. Later, no one would agree how it began, and in the heart of the crowd it was impossible to tell. Were the missiles thrown first or did they fly in reaction to something that had happened, something we could not see? Two bottles collided in mid-air and showered those beneath with brown and green glass. It did not seem possible but the crowd grew tighter. A surge from the front. A surge from the back. The helicopter hovered lower, and I could feel the warm air being pushed down by its rotor blades, until more flying bottles forced it to move away and out of range. We need to go, I thought. We need to go, I said. K. agreed. She was still holding my hand. We tried to move back through the crowd, back in the direction from which we'd originally come and away from the black smoke, rising in a column. We made it about fifty metres back down the street, and then the moment came.

We were holding hands, and then we weren't. We were together, and then we weren't. We were packed in tight, and suddenly we were released.

It was like a gate had opened. The crowd moved forward at such speed that people slipped and fell. Almost immediately

I lost K., but at this point I was not worried. If anything, the sudden release of pressure on the crowd made me feel sure I was going to get out of there and away. And then, another surge from behind. A scream. Panic now. Turning my head, I could see a moving wall of black. The first sighting of a baton and a shield, used not for defence but as a battering ram. I looked for K. but there was no sign. Later, I would have the vision of a man's face, right in front of mine, until he was no longer there, replaced by a helmet and my own face reflected back at me, the man crumpled at my feet. I felt the air move with the next baton swing, aimed in my direction. It missed, just.

It was loud now, with shouts and screams, bangs and sirens. I could see a gap ahead, where the police lines had broken, leading to a space between two apartment buildings. I tried to move towards it, tried to dodge the pockets of police, tried to ignore the soft landings when my feet came down on something other than hot tarmac. On the edge of the crowd I turned to look back; saw the crowd of protestors and police intermingled, the separation into strange pockets of almost peaceful calm and frenzied violence, only a few metres from each other. The apartment block residents watched from the safety of their balconies as the battle raged beneath them. There was no sign of K. I saw a column of police moving along the side in my direction, and tried to find a place where I could scan the crowd but avoid contact with their batons or with their shields.

And then a shout.

K., behind me, next to a tree.

She guided me between the buildings, to the back of the apartment blocks and their car parks and playgrounds.

PAUL SCRATON

Almost immediately, the sound of the battle retreated, cut off from where we stood by the twelve-storey walls of the socialist-era housing blocks. A man crossed the car park with two bags of shopping, nodding at us as he made his way to his building. We looked each other up and down. My T-shirt was ripped, but otherwise I was fine. K. had a bluish bruise already forming on her face. She did not remember receiving the blow.

We moved away, following side streets north until we were a long way clear of the demonstration route. K. was trying Tomas on his mobile phone but there was no connection. Just a couple of blocks from Karl-Marx-Allee and the city was as normal. Children on the swings in the playground. Drunks passing bottles on the steps by the Spanish Civil War memorial. We debated what to do. My apartment was only a block from the planned demonstration route. It seemed unwise to go back in that direction. K. had left her keys at our place, so there was no way we could go to hers. We stuck to our plan, and began the twenty-minute walk to the beer garden.

Later, on the news, there was footage of the fight, filmed by crews both down in the crowds and up on the balconies, overlooking the scene. The journalists delivered their pieces to camera, after the event, on empty streets strewn with discarded banners and fallen helmets, broken bottles and all the other debris of what had gone on before. They made their first reports while we were still walking to the beer garden, making declarations about what had happened well before any real facts could possibly have emerged. On all sides, stories were being straightened, as the fault and blame began to be laid at the feet of others.

K.'s phone signal returned at the gates of the beer garden. She took her first call as we followed the short path down the side of the theatre to the chestnut trees and the ranks of yellow tables and benches. It was Boris. He was driving back to the city. There'd been a call on his phone. I watched K.'s face change as she heard the news, watched it shift and distort as she listened to what he was telling her. The colour, gone from her cheeks. The light, deadened in her eyes. We turned and made our way to the hospital. Tried to get in, to get some answers, to find out what was going on, but the scene was so chaotic that we only found out we had been sent to the wrong place many hours later. It wouldn't have mattered. Tomas had died long before he made it to any hospital, in the ambulance, as it tried to force its way through the crowds.

The smell of the river on a hot summer evening.

K. and I sat on the embankment waiting for Boris. When he arrived we sat and held each other. None of us cried. Not yet. It was too early. We still didn't believe it. Boris had spoken to Tomas's parents, who were on their way from Sweden. The police had told them he had hit his head. It would later emerge that he had banged his head on the police van, in the process of being arrested. Accident. Deliberate. Negligent. Whatever the official files would say later, everyone had their own opinion as to how Tomas died. Those who had been with Tomas told anyone who would listen that he had done nothing to justify an arrest. He was just swept up, perhaps because he was the one holding the megaphone. At least two newspapers, the following day, printed allegations from unnamed police sources that Tomas had attacked a police officer and was struggling when they tried to get him into the van. This evidence was never presented, and where the information came from was never made clear. But even if Tomas had not been to blame, the accident that caused his death was, it seemed to be agreed, caused by the violence of the protestors as a whole. The response, online and in the later protests that continued throughout the long, hot summer, was that Tomas had been killed by the police during an unprovoked attack on a peaceful demonstration.

It took a while for them to release the body. We travelled to Sweden for the funeral, driving north to Rostock in Boris's Skoda. On the ferry, K. slept in the cabin while I got drunk in the bar. Boris kept me company, sober ahead of the drive next morning. I told him, as the ferry rolled beneath us, that I wanted to drink enough to forget. He told me he was staying sober to remember. Not much would remain about the days that followed. Some words, uttered by a person whose name and face I no longer recall.

His eyes were as blue as a mountain lake.

The sound of birds outside the chapel. The sun reflecting on the photographers' lenses. A German tabloid and a morbid desire for pictures of the funeral. I remember feeling happy, for their sake, that Boris left the service early.

On the night Tomas died, K. returned with Boris and me to the apartment. As we entered, Boris moved ahead to close Tomas's bedroom door, and we only opened it again a few days later, when his parents came to gather his things. We sat at the kitchen table and drank wine and whisky, looking down onto the empty street, the usual parked cars still absent, where we had seen the columns of police walking in step only that morning. It felt like another decade. Boris went to bed first, leaving K. and me sitting at the table. The bruise on her face had turned angry, but it wasn't swollen.

She leaned across the table to kiss me on the lips. I could feel her sadness. Then she kissed me again, more urgently, lifting her hands to my head. She did not want to go home alone, she said. She asked me if she could stay. Wordlessly, I agreed, and she led me to my bedroom. As we undressed, she moved close, placing her hand on my chest.

'I want to feel alive,' she said.

It was the end. It was the beginning.

On the hottest of Berlin's summer days, we would talk about Tomas. We would talk about our memories of him as a flatmate and a friend, of the sound of his voice and the stories he loved to tell. We would remember that day, and how we had felt on Karl-Marx-Allee, on the walk to the beer garden and on the banks of the river. For a long time it seemed the only way to process those few hours and what we experienced together. What we never spoke about was what happened next, what happened that night.

The next morning, we ate breakfast in near silence

and then, when Boris emerged, we tried to work out the practicalities of what we were supposed to do next. We had no preparation, no family nearby. We only had each other, and that could not last, not completely and not forever. K. and I would often speak of Tomas and the day he died, but we never managed to speak of what had happened in my room that night. We did not speak about it in the early weeks and months, as we built a relationship and tried to grieve our friend, and then it seemed as if too much time had passed. The risk was too great. What could be gained? So, the great silence of that moment remained between us until the end, even if I could forever picture K. above me, moving slowly in the shadows cast by the lights shining in through the bedroom window from the empty street beyond.

X

Spindrift

The hotel room window looked out over the market square of a small town in northern Brandenburg, halfway between Berlin and the Baltic. It was late afternoon, early in the year, and the sky above the rooftops was already dark. The snow, which had been falling for nearly two days, had blanketed the square and the pavements, covering roofs and clinging to the outstretched branches of trees. On the street, car tyres ploughed two furrows along which other vehicles could make careful progress, but no one was driving unless they absolutely had to. In the corner of the room, news bulletins showed images of cars stranded on the motorway, headlights illuminating the snow as it fell in front of the beams, the windscreen wipers impotently pushing the flakes away. The scene shifted to a wildlife park in Mecklenburg, where the elephants roamed across a snow-covered enclosure. It was, the newsreader intoned over the images, the storm of the century. Northern and eastern Germany was frozen, locked in place. Supermarkets stood empty as deliveries failed to arrive. Volunteers carried coal to the houses of their elderly neighbours, to fill the ovens in the corner of each room. If it continued, the emergency services had warned, people were going to lose their lives. In the hotel room, the television screen and the view from the window told the story. Otherwise, no words were exchanged.

We were trapped, halfway home from a trip to the coast that we had taken to gain space and distance, and time to make plans. We had walked the promenade of the off-season holiday resort and looked down at the snow-covered beach. By the time the warnings came of a worsening in the weather and we made hasty plans to return to Berlin, nothing had been resolved. We caught the train as the wind swirled the snow down the platform and the waves battered the pier beyond the beach. We made it to the market town before news came over the loudspeaker that power lines were down and the tracks were blocked. We were stranded. A few hours later, from the hotel room, I could see the snow had finally stopped. The wind had died away. We would be able to return to Berlin the following morning.

A conversation from the previous evening hung in the room between us, as K. lay on the bed flicking between channels and I stared out of the window. I would come to see those days as the turning point, as the start of a conversation that would take another year or so to reach its conclusion. On the coast, I had looked out across choppy waters and seen a Baltic as unsettled as I had ever witnessed it before. The sky above was grey and moody. Sandbags had been piled up against the wooden beach bar at the end of the pier. As the storm approached, the cafes and restaurants that were still open in the off-season closed their shutters and sent their staff home. It all suited my mood. The mood between us.

I left the hotel room and went for a walk, crunching along the pavement as gusts of wind dislodged miniature snowdrifts from gables and window ledges, dusting my hat and jacket as I passed beneath. With the storm finally over, others were also out, braving the cold. A smoker standing outside the town centre's solitary bar pulled on a cigarette, his jacket turned up high around his neck. He watched me as I walked by, and I could feel his eyes on me as I moved further down the street. A taxi cruised slowly along the road between us, orange light glowing on the roof, searching for the right address. A young woman stepped out onto the pavement from an apartment building a few metres ahead of me, wrapped up against the cold, her breath visible as she talked into the phone she held to her ear. Her voice, as it carried along the pavement, sounded strange in the otherwise muffled town. Her problems, as she relayed them, had not been swallowed by the snow.

I was walking with no destination in mind at the very moment I should have been in the hotel room with K. She had not looked up from the television screen when I told her I was going out, asked no questions and made no requests. As I opened the door I knew that it was a mistake, but I had stepped out into the landing, which smelled of old cigarettes and lavender air freshener, and walked to the stairs regardless. On the street of the snow-covered market town I stopped in the shadow of a red-brick Gothic church, seemingly built in stages, and tried to see if I could imagine the story of the building simply through its different layers of stone.

My problem, K. told me once, was that I seemed to be more interested in ghosts than in the living.

A path took me along the route of the old city walls, between a row of cottages and the medieval brickwork. On the other side, where the moat had once been, a green strip of grass, chestnut and walnut trees had been allowed to grow, the snow-covered branches easily breaching the town's ancient defences. I kept walking, the path along the walls offering me a purpose now, a destination in mind and a circle to complete. My fingers were chilled, and I pushed them deep into my pockets, but otherwise it didn't feel that cold. Not if I kept moving, step by step, passing more houses, towers and gateways as I went, as well as the signs for competing discount supermarkets that guarded opposite ends of the old town, just beyond the walls.

I saw the woman from across a small square. She was standing in an illuminated room at the base of one of the gatehouses in the city walls. The only person in there, she was looking down at something on the table in front of her, glasses resting on the end of her nose. A sign, blasted by snow and wind, was just about able to communicate that the town museum would be open for another hour. As I moved closer to get a better look, the automatic glass doors slid open, causing the woman to look up from whatever she was doing and greet me with a smile. There was no longer any choice. I felt the warm air hit me as I stepped inside, the smell of electric heaters mixed with the damp that lived in the centuries-old brickwork.

Frau Grautoff welcomed me with her name, which I could also read on the badge pinned to her chest, and a request for my postcode, for their records. She told me that the day had been surprisingly quiet, as if she had somehow missed the apocalyptic storm that had been swirling outside, but that she was glad to have someone to show around. Of course, I was more than welcome to explore the museum on my own, Frau Grautoff continued, but in her experience visitors got more out of it when she or one of her colleagues was on hand to provide a little more detail, a little context, about what it was they were looking at. In actual fact, she said, lowering her voice, if she was being honest, the person who had put together the exhibits in the museum had done it in a particularly ramshackle way, and it would be highly unlikely that I would be able to make proper sense of it on my own. I agreed she should lead the way.

She began with the maps, a series of five prints hanging on the wall that told the story of the old town centre, from its origins as a medieval marketplace to the snow-covered, sleepy provincial outpost I had been walking through that afternoon. The key to understanding the story of the town, Frau Grautoff insisted, was through its destruction. The history of this place was defined by a handful of cataclysmic events, all of which involved fire. There was a bakery fire, which had grown out of hand and wiped out the old wooden houses that had originally stood within the town walls. Then there was a deliberate fire, an act of criminal arson, perpetrated by a marauding army at the end of the Thirty Years War. Although they had destroyed the town, Frau Grautoff expressed sympathy for the hungry soldiers. They were a long way from home, cut adrift once the fighting had stopped, and traumatised by what they had experienced. Although she could never be sure, Frau Grautoff believed that they hadn't intended to burn down the entire town, just the house of one of the locals who had refused them food and shelter for the night. Another story had it that they had started the fire because they had not been granted access to the grain stores. Or perhaps it was because the grain stores were empty. The stories, as they tended to do, she continued, varied immensely. It didn't really matter why the fire was started, only that it was, and that it spread quickly. The town burned once more.

There were more fires, later, but as the wooden houses were replaced by those made of stone, the fires became smaller, less dramatic and more easily contained. That was, of course, until the British bombers flew over on their way home from Berlin. With a few bombs left, having attempted to destroy their principal targets in the capital of the Third Reich, they dropped what remained on the town. Somehow the church survived, and the medieval walls, but much of the rest of the town was laid to waste.

Frau Grautoff was not a religious woman, she said, and she never had been. Even as a child, the stories to be found in the Bible seemed so unlikely. And yet, through all the fires and the bombs, the church had survived. What were we to make of that?

She looked at me expectantly, and when I shrugged, she turned away, back to the maps, disappointed.

Look, she continued, running her hand along the wall beneath the five maps in their simple, wooden frames. What did I notice about them, these five maps that covered seven hundred years of the town's history? I wondered if Frau Grautoff had been a schoolteacher in a previous life, or at a previous moment in this one. She looked triumphant as I mumbled an answer.

Yes!

The town, she said, pointing at each map in turn, had always been built to the same street plan, every time it was destroyed. Despite the fires and the marauding armies, the bombs and, later, the busybody communist planners from Berlin, despite the fact that over those seven hundred years almost every building within the town walls had been built, destroyed and rebuilt, sometimes many times over, in some ways the town was still exactly the same. The man who drew that very first map would be able to find his way through the town today. It all linked together, she said, via the pathways and lanes that over centuries had been followed by people and horses, carts and cars, carriages and buses.

She clapped her hands together.

'I could look at these maps for hours,' she said.

Instead, she pulled herself way, leading me through to the back room where the museum curator had, in no particular chronological, epochal or thematic order, gathered together the artefacts of everyday life in the town. Farming implements and hunting equipment, nets and baskets from the long history of fishing in the surrounding rivers and lakes, and bits and pieces from the workshops of the early Industrial Revolution.

The town was never destined to grow, Frau Grautoff said. At one point in time, the population was the same as that of Berlin. But these things are a matter of geography and politics, of nature and luck. Every time the population swelled, it declined again. War and emigration. Changes elsewhere, pulling people away. To other cities and countries, or to the coast and across the ocean to a New World beyond.

We picked our way through the things that had been left behind. Mandolins and pipes, card games and sets of porcelain cups, sewing kits and cigar boxes. Most of what they had, Frau Grautoff continued, had been sourced from the town itself. People had searched through their attics and basements, dropping things off at the library where the council had made storage space available to them. They had hoped that these contributions would build a connection between the people of the town and the museum, to make them want to engage with what was being done. But for the most part they never came, she said sadly, they never visited to see what had been done with their things.

Nevertheless, she still believed it was important that the museum was there. Preserving a link to the past, to the stories of the town.

She led me across to a cabinet by her desk, which she unlocked before bending down to lift out, from behind the glass, a postcard and a photograph. The latter was a picture of a young woman, with attractive features and dark curly hair that framed her face. She was smiling ever so slightly as she looked at the camera, as if she knew a secret that she was not yet willing to tell. The postcard was of a town square, somewhere in central Europe. It could have been any number of places, but the letters printed at the bottom of the card made it all clear.

THERESIENSTADT.

I turned it over to see scrawled handwriting and an address, somewhere in the United States.

It was written, Frau Grautoff said, from inside the walls of the ghetto concentration camp and sent across the ocean to a sister living in America. Before she had begun her work at the museum, Frau Grautoff had never imagined that those who had been held at Theresienstadt would have been allowed to send postcards. It seemed too normal an act.

She took both pieces of card from my hands.

The woman in the photograph was called Maja, she said, and it was Maja who wrote the postcard. When the photograph was taken she would have been nineteen or twenty. Whenever Frau Grautoff looked at the photograph, looked at Maja, she couldn't help but think she must have been a nice young woman. Someone to be friends with.

She bent down and put the cards back in place and locked the cabinet once more.

The town never had a large Jewish population, she continued, as she went back to her desk. In 1801, there had been seven families. In 1815, their records showed a total of between thirty-five and forty individuals. By 1925, the number had fallen again, down to six.

Frau Grautoff shrugged.

There were a number of reasons for this, she continued. The overall population of the town had shrunk during the second half of the nineteenth century. Lots of people, Jewish or otherwise, had left for Berlin, for elsewhere in Germany, or to London, or New York. It was the same today, she said. The attraction of the big city, the jobs or the excitement. The bright lights. Sometimes, on a clear night, she would stand at the southern gate of the old town and she could see the glow of Berlin in the distance. Today, it still called their young people away, and only some of them would return.

PAUL SCRATON

In 1925, Maja had been one of the six. Her parents, two sisters and a younger brother were the rest. She was the oldest of the siblings, and in 1932 she married a local man, one of their neighbours growing up. He had been away to Berlin but returned to the town to set up a lawyer's practice, and by all accounts theirs was a happy marriage. Religion was not something that mattered to either of them, nor to their respective families. But it was less than a year after the wedding that Hitler came to power. It must have been a shock, Frau Grautoff said. Many didn't leave, but Maja's father was one of the first. He had a brother in America, a successful merchant, who was able to sponsor a visa. The family had enough money for tickets and he had no desire to stick around and see what was to develop. Within a couple of months of the Nazis gaining power in Berlin, they had gone. A train to the capital and then on to Hamburg. A boat to Liverpool. From Liverpool to New York.

Except, Frau Grautoff conceded, it was not all of them. Maja stayed behind with her husband. By 1933, the number of Jews in the town had fallen to exactly one. Perhaps it was this that meant it took a while for them to come for her. But come for her they did. In 1944, with her husband away, fighting in the east, Maja was put on a train. First to Berlin, then to Theresienstadt. It was while she was being held in the camp that her husband was killed. While she was there, her home town was destroyed by British bombs. Her family, now settled in the United States, were desperately worried about her. But incredible as it was to say it in that way, Maja was one of the 'lucky' ones. She survived. When the camps were liberated and the gates opened, she was still alive.

Her husband was dead. From Theresienstadt she was able, with her father's help, to travel to America, reuniting with her parents, brother and sisters on the quayside in New York. They lived in New Jersey, where her father owned a bookshop and her mother had just completed her qualifications to be a kindergarten teacher. They had a room for her in the house and a job for her in the shop. The paperwork would be no problem. Like them, she would be an American in no time. But on that first evening in New Jersey, Maja told her family her plans. She was only there for a visit. She fully intended to return home. To the devastated town where she had grown up and fallen in love. Her town. Her husband's town. And so she did. After 1949, she was a citizen of the German Democratic Republic, but her status as a Holocaust survivor meant she was allowed to travel, to see her family in the United States. And she did, quite often, but she was determined to remain in Germany.

'I have told this story many times,' Frau Grautoff said, 'But I am still...'

She did not have the word, but I knew what she was trying to say.

Maja died in 1963. Frau Grautoff thought that she might have been forgotten, if it wasn't for one of the museum volunteers who found a newspaper cutting about Maja from the time of her return to the town at the end of the war. There was attention, then, in those early years, as if people needed a positive story as they came to terms with the crimes that had been committed in their names. But of course, Frau Grautoff continued, Maja was the exception. That's what made her a story. And she was an exception two times over, as a survivor and a returnee. We should not think of her story as typical.

Sometimes, Frau Grautoff wished she could have met Maja, to ask her what she thought about her friends and neighbours when she returned to the town, about what she thought they had known. Where did they think Maja had been taken? And yet, from everything Frau Grautoff had read, Maja rekindled many old friendships on her return. How could she have done that, seemingly with such feeling and good grace?

Frau Grautoff shook her head.

She supposed that part of the story no longer mattered. Most of them, including Maja, were long dead. Most of their names were forgotten. But not Maja's. We still had her name, her photograph, and the postcard that told us where she had been and, without needing to write it down, what it was she had seen. The picture and the photographs had been sent to them by a nephew. He lived in Massachusetts, and had learned of the museum and the desire to honour Maja in some way. He was old himself now, and unable to travel for the opening. He apologised, but said he hoped the photograph and the postcard would allow his aunt to be remembered in her home town for a long time to come.

We stood for a moment longer, looking down at the cabinet and the view across the square at Theresienstadt, as Maja smiled back at us.

As I left the museum, Frau Grautoff asked me when I would be travelling back to Berlin. It would be nice, she said, if before I left I went to see the cranes. It used to be unheard of, for the cranes to be here in winter. Her father used to keep a record of their migrations. But now, for a couple of years at least, some were hanging around. She told me that I should follow the town walls to the Powder Gate and then walk across the supermarket car park. They liked to gather on the field beyond, striding across the cold, frozen ground. So elegant.

'I could watch them for hours,' she said.

K. was in the hotel restaurant when I got back, reading from a heavy, hardback book that lay open on the table in front of her, next to a glass of wine and a plate containing the remnants of her dinner. She had been hungry, she said, and hadn't known when I was returning. I sat next to her. She continued to read, but under the table she took my hand and gave it a squeeze. It was going to be all right, she seemed to be saying, and at that moment I deeply wished it would prove to be true.

As she read on, I drank a beer and waited for some food of my own, thinking of Frau Grautoff and the museum, thinking about Maja. It was a beautiful name. There was a sadness about her photograph. It was not just because of the story as Frau Grautoff told it, but because old photographs in general had a tendency to make me sad, especially when they introduced me to someone I would have loved to meet but which time and space had made impossible. Maja looked like someone to be friends with. I agreed with Frau Grautoff about that.

Later, as K. slept, I climbed out of bed to go over to the window. I thought it had started to snow again, but as I got closer I realised it was not fresh snow falling but that which had landed earlier, gathered on the roof above and disturbed now by a sudden gust of wind, deep into the witching hour. I looked out of the window and saw my reflection. K. sleeping, both in the middle of the square and in the bed behind me. As I looked, I wondered how many hotel rooms we had left.

As the old snow was blown from the roof to fall beyond the window, seemingly between the glass and our reflection, it looked as if K. and I were trapped in a snow globe, one which had been given a good shake and had not yet begun to settle. I moved closer to the window, resting my forehead against the glass so that the room behind me disappeared from view. Now it was just me and the town. Frau Grautoff's town. Maja's town. I was facing south, and so I looked to the sky beyond the buildings at the opposite side of the square. I looked for the glow of Berlin. But that night at least, the lights of the city were not shining brightly enough.

XI

Lost Lane

On Lost Lane there were two lines of cherry blossom trees, planted in an overgrown space between the pavement and the brick walls that once supported railway lines on their journey from the city to the coast. The trees had been a gift, a present from the other side of the world, and they stood there as a symbol of the days of change that had been broadcast across the time zones. As revolutions went, 1989 was a particularly televisual one, as pictures of wall-dancers and toppling statues, round-table discussions and firing squads, were broadcast across the continents. It seemed fitting that of all the sites of memory that could be found along the former border of the once-divided city, it was these cherry blossom trees, paid for by a television station, that were the most striking of all.

In April, when leading tours along Lost Lane, I would stop beneath the first pinks and whites that had burst from the gnarled and twisted branches above the pavement. I would tell the story of the fall of the Wall and a Japanese television campaign, a million dollars raised and nine thousand trees to replace concrete slabs and wire fences that had only so recently been removed.

There were other stories along Lost Lane. When Rike K. lived there, her bedroom window looked out across the street to railway tracks that had already become the boundary between the Soviet and French sectors of the city, but had not yet been ripped up and replaced by the fortified border. In those post-war years, with the two sides defined but the dividing line still open, she would cross beneath the tracks via a long tunnel that took her from Lost Lane to the neighbourhood on the other side. Rike used the tunnel to visit her aunt, to go shopping or for a trip to the movies. Her aunt would cross in the opposite direction to buy books and recordings of classical music, for a night at the opera or a trip to the theatre. At that time the sector boundaries were patrolled, and suspicious pedestrians might be checked, but in general the way to the other side was open, whether by tunnel or by bridge, or simply by crossing the street.

The border had still not been closed when Rike K. turned eighteen and was offered a place to study in Denmark. She had never left the German Democratic Republic, except to visit the western half of her home city, and she was excited about the possibility of a few years abroad. Why Denmark? Rike had no proper answer, other than a desire to see new things and experience new places. She was eighteen. What other reason did she need? When she was asked later, when her story was known, something to be repeated, she still didn't have an answer that convinced even her. Why Denmark? Why not? It was simply 'somewhere else', and that would have to do.

With a letter from Copenhagen in her hand, she applied for an exit visa. The application was denied. She tried again and was denied again. She discussed the situation with her mother and with her aunt on the other side, but with no one else. Even in those early days, when the border was not yet a physical barrier, she knew she had to be careful who she spoke to. Should she apply again? Keep applying? No. She decided she'd had enough. Rike K. made a plan. She would walk beneath the railway tracks, following the tunnel from Lost Lane to the neighbourhood beyond, a walk she had made many, many times. Only this time, she was not coming back.

She could have done it there and then, but there were things she wanted to take with her, things she felt she needed. And so, she arranged a series of evening meals with her aunt on the other side. Every Friday for twelve weeks, she crossed beneath the tracks with a simple cotton shopping bag on her shoulder. Later that evening she would return, the shopping bag folded in her pocket. On the thirteenth Friday, she looked out of her window across Lost Lane for the final time, kissed her mother goodbye, and walked out of the house and down to the entrance to the tunnel.

'If they had simply let me go to Copenhagen,' she would say, many years later, 'I am sure I would have come back. It never occurred to me to leave forever, until they wanted to stop me going in the first place.'

On the thirteenth Friday evening, she walked through the tunnel for the last time, and said goodbye to the GDR for good.

After Copenhagen she moved to London, for love and a marriage that would not last, before returning to Germany and a small village outside Aachen, close to the Belgian and Dutch borders. It was while she was still in Denmark that the tunnel linking Lost Lane to the West was closed. The railway lines were ripped up and barbed wire fence rolled out along the entire length of the border. Soon there would be concrete walls and trip wires, guard towers, guns and a shoot-to-kill order. Rike K.'s mother had been with her sister in the West on the night the border was closed, and she decided to stay put. She moved on to Cologne, and the apartment on Lost Lane, abandoned with the building of the Berlin Wall, was soon emptied out and rented to others, those who could be trusted with a bedroom view of the border and its fortifications.

Neither Rike K. nor her mother would return to Lost Lane until long after the fall of the Wall and the wire, the concrete and the watchtowers had been taken away.

'I did not think I could face it,' she said. 'Not before all traces were gone.'

But it was impossible to remove them all. There would come a time when the Wall had been down longer than it was ever up, but traces would remain. It continued to be written into the very fabric of the city.

At the entrance to the tunnel on Lost Lane, a sign would swing in the breeze above where yellow bricks had been used to close it off during the years of division.

IN. OUT. IN. OUT.

Above the tunnel, where the railway lines had been removed to create the no man's land of the Wall, a scruffy park of patchy grass and slender silver birches had replaced the raked sand and trip wires of the border. I had walked through the park many times, crossing over from one side to the other using the tunnel, passing through its cool, gloomy interior, where it was possible to still hear the echoes of metal wheels on metal tracks and the engine sounds of a border guard's jeep, Rike K.'s footsteps on a Friday evening and the crack of gunshot on a cold January night.

It was called Lost Lane because that had once been a name, marked on old maps created long before the arrival of the railway lines that would flank it, back when the city walls were away to the south and the road passed through a landscape of meadows and marshland, glacial lakes and forests. The *Verlorener Weg* was a sandy trail, rutted and slow, and it got the name because it belonged to no one: no estate or settlement, no town or village. It was forsaken and doomed, damned and lost. There were many Lost Lanes dug into the sandy soil of Prussia, and as it became understood that nowhere truly belonged to no one, and that the lanes were no longer lost, they were renamed. The Lost Lane of Rike K. and the cherry blossom trees was swallowed up as the city spread out to the north and laid a claim to it, with the railway lines on one side and rows of working-class tenement blocks on the other. It was all part of a grand plan to turn a garrison town into a global city, one which paved over the meadows, buried the rivers and overwhelmed medieval villages with hundreds of new streets and avenues, all of which needed names. And so they were named in clusters. Poets and conductors, places in Scandinavia or Britain or elsewhere in Germany.

Lost Lane, now a city street, was named for a small town on the western bank of the River Oder that would find itself a border town, facing Poland across the river, at the very moment Lost Lane followed the border in the heart of Berlin. Boundaries had shifted once more, as old maps were used to create new ones, and an administrative boundary marked by railway lines, of interest only to civil servants and postal workers, became a dividing line between two competing ideologies.

There was a story that the phrase *wrong side of the tracks* came from the United States and the expansion of the railways in the time of steam engines. Prevailing winds would cause more soot, on average, to land on one side of a town than the other. Thus, those who could afford it would build their houses upwind, and leave the poor to deal with the pollution. The wrong side was the dirty side. Etymologists disputed this theory, arguing that smoke from factories and the fireplaces in ordinary homes would have created far more airborne pollution than infrequently passing trains, but the idea of the railway tracks as an economic dividing line stuck. Prosperity versus poverty. Tranquillity versus chaos. Peaceful evenings on the porch versus the rat-a-tat-tat of gunfire and the howl of the sirens that it summoned.

On Lost Lane, the railway lines originally ran between two neighbourhoods of equal deprivation, of shared poverty, pollution and the political radicalism they gave birth to. Before the war and the building of the Berlin Wall, both neighbourhoods were red, electing socialists and communists to the Reichstag even after the country around them was increasingly stained in brown. It was only later, after the tracks were ripped up and it became a border, that the neighbourhoods diverged. And three decades after the Wall came down, and the cherry blossoms bloomed for the first time, there remained two very different neighbourhoods at either end of the tunnel.

IN. OUT. IN. OUT.

In the spring of my penultimate year in the city, I was walking down Lost Lane when I heard a shout from across the street. At first, I did not think the shout was directed at me, but still I turned to see Boris waving from a first-floor window, a few houses down from where Rike K. had once lived. We hadn't seen each other since the day of Otto's funeral. Numbers had changed, social media accounts had been deleted. I had heard from mutual friends that he was still in Berlin. I heard from others that he had given up on Berlin, and that he had left for good. That he had gone home.

I didn't believe them, for Boris always said that his home no longer existed.

'The names might still be there,' he had said. 'On the map, or train timetables. But if you go there, you won't find them. Not really. However hard you look.'

Now, as he stood at the window, bare-chested and beckoning me across the street, he was smiling and the years seemed to fall away. There was no distance between us, he seemed to say, not in this moment. Not yet. I crossed Lost

Lane and as I stepped up onto the pavement beneath his window, he disappeared. He was going to the apartment door and would be waiting for me to press the bell, so he could buzz me up.

*

On one of our final trips out of the city in Boris's old Skoda, we had passed through the town on the Oder that gave Lost Lane its name. We had taken a trip to Poland, for cheap cigarettes for Boris and bottles of vodka we planned to share. If we wanted, we could have also stopped for cut-price wedding dresses, tyres for the Skoda, or a cheap haircut at the bazaar which stretched out along the road just after we'd crossed the river and into another country. We cruised through the border town on the German side of the river as we were making our way home, looking out through the car windows at a place transformed after the Second World War from a sleepy market town to an industrial zone with a huge oil refinery, paper mill and line after line of concrete-slab apartment blocks to house the people to work in them. Almost overnight, the population of the town increased fivefold, as workers arrived from across the GDR to start their new lives in the town on the border.

We drove through the town more than two decades after reunification, and we could feel the impact of what had followed. The GDR-era apartment blocks were being dismantled, leaving wide streets and empty spaces. With the workforce greatly reduced following the privatisation of the town's industries, people had left to seek new opportunities elsewhere, in the same way as they had come to the town in the first place.

Expand, contract. In, out.

It would not be long until the town had returned to its pre-war population, with most traces of the GDR replaced with the empty spaces where the apartment blocks, schools and shopping halls had once stood. In those twenty-five years there had been other changes, too. The border to Poland was now open, and a new bridge linked the town with their neighbours on the other side. Then the border guards left and the brand new checkpoints shuttered beneath blue European flags, as traffic moved back and forth across the bridge without hindrance, from the red and white border posts on one side to the black-red-gold on the other.

We had stopped by the river to look across, as Boris smoked a Polish cigarette on the German riverbank.

'All those places over there once had German names,' he said, as he smoked. They still did in his road atlas, he continued, even though it had only been published a year or so before. But in all those villages, the population had changed, in some cases from one day to the next. He wondered if people had come to the riverbank in those early years, to look across the water and try to catch a glimpse of their old village, their old church spire or even their old farmhouse. Did they come to look across, even in the knowledge that they would never return? That was thing about home, he continued. It was not really a place. A name on a map or a road atlas. It was a feeling. A moment in time or the words of a song. The continued use of a language or the slow development of a family recipe as it altered to new circumstances. It existed, he insisted, and it was real. The town, the landscape... But if it existed, it could also cease to exist. It could disappear, and it could be taken away.

✳

Boris stood at the window, once again looking down onto Lost Lane as I perched on the arm of a sofa in the corner of his living room. Of all the apartments Boris lived in during his time in Berlin, this was the smallest, but there were many reminders of the others. The bookshelves, which filled one whole wall of the living room, seemed to have been transplanted exactly as they were. The schoolroom map of the Socialist Federal Republic of Yugoslavia faced them across the room. By the window was a small desk, above which hung the film poster for *Rani radovi*, with its additional dialogue by Karl Marx and Friedrich Engels.

From the corner of the room, I asked Boris the questions friends ask when they have not seen each other for a while. I asked him about work and the apartment. About friends we had in common and about his film project. I asked him if it was finished.

'It's over there,' he said, nodding at a pile of shoeboxes stacked neatly on the bottom of one of the bookshelves, a name stencilled on each side. *Early Works #1, Early Works #2…* A list of contents taped to each lid. He hadn't looked at them since he moved in, he continued, looking at the boxes from across the room with narrowed eyes, as if he was seeing them for the first time.

'I don't know if they are worth anything.'

He changed the subject, asking if I was still doing the tours, still repeating the same old stories, dwelling on the dark and troubled past of the city. I sensed he was gently mocking me, and as he talked I remembered how tired conversations with Boris could make me, and how those long nights beneath the poster for *Rani radovi* would invariably end. I could have answered him properly, but I didn't have the energy. I muttered something about how it continued to pay the rent.

'Something must,' he conceded, turning back to look out of the window. 'And how is Karolina?'

His use of K.'s full name pulled me up short. Had he always used it? Since childhood, even within her family, she had been known as K. Hadn't it always been Tomas who called her Karolina? I doubted my memory. Perhaps it had been Boris all along.

She was fine, I told him, but that wasn't a proper answer either. I changed the subject, asking more questions about the apartment, about whether he still liked living in the neighbourhood, despite all the changes.

He picked at the peeling paint on the window frame.

'I like the sunsets,' he said. 'The cherry blossom in spring. The girls on their bikes in the summer.'

He laughed. It didn't matter, he continued, whether he liked it or not because they were raising the rent. Not by much, but enough. I asked him where he would go but he didn't know. Since he arrived in Berlin, he had always lived in this neighbourhood. They'd pushed him over time, further north and right to the very edge, and now he had nowhere else to go. He nodded in the direction of the houses on the other side, past Lost Lane and the cherry blossom trees, the silver birches and the park.

'Maybe I'll move over there,' he said, distaste in his voice; and, as if unwilling to contemplate this any further, he moved away from the window and stood by the map on the wall, the towns and cities linked by roads and railway lines and rivers, the names of places made famous by the shattered peace that the map represented.

He'd had an idea for a film once, Boris said as he stood beneath his map. It was about a piece of fencing. A tangle of barbed wire, or perhaps just a simple piece of fencing, like you would use to close off an electrical substation or a tennis court. In the story, the fencing would have originally stood in Berlin, used as part of the border that divided the city until 1989, when it was no longer needed. The 1990s in Germany were nothing if not the environmental decade, and so it was decided to recycle their border, selling the fencing to one of the new Yugoslav republics after independence, so they could close off their newly recognised international boundaries from their former brothers and sisters.

He traced a finger along a dotted red line between Croatia and Bosnia-Herzegovina.

As one came down, another went up, he said. They needed the fence, right when the others didn't. But the story did not end there. There always had to be a third act. And so, at the end of the journey the fence moves again. Things have settled down between the old neighbours, and the fence is once again no longer needed. So they sell it to their neighbours to the east, who need to protect those borders ever more strongly, now that they have been admitted into the European club. A city, a country, a continent. The borders don't disappear, he said, they simply move.

He rubbed his face.

'It would have to be,' he said, thoughtfully, 'I don't know... surreal as fuck.'

I asked him what happened to the idea.

'The fence?' he said, looking at me, as if he hadn't just spent a couple of minutes outlining the idea. 'I've no idea. It's probably over there, in one of those boxes. But like I said, I haven't opened any of them in years.'

Half an hour later, I left the apartment. Boris walked me to the door. Standing on the landing, as he leaned against the door frame, I suggested we meet up sometime, for a drink. Maybe after he had moved, once he was settled.

'Not any more,' he said, his voice soft, as he looked down at the red, worn carpet on the landing. I took it to mean he had stopped drinking, that he had reached the end of that particular road, but deep down I knew that it was also a simple recognition of the truth. There was little point. Things had drifted on too long for us. There was nothing left.

I stepped out onto Lost Lane in the spring sunshine, and followed it to where the street gave way to a bridge that lifted the bike path up and over the S-Bahn tracks. To the left, in the former border strip, huge cranes swung against the blue sky, working to build new student housing that would cost more per a month for a studio flat than entire families paid for their apartments in my neighbourhood. By then, it had also become clear to us that K. and I were only holding on because we had stayed put, just about hanging on to our place in the city, safe as long as we did not flinch. Our protection was in the apartment and the rental contract we had. If we were to leave, that would be it. There would be no coming back.

As I walked up the bridge, someone had tied flowers to the railings, hanging there above a collection of red glass candle holders. Inside one, a flame flickered, but the rest had long been extinguished. In that big city, the news or story had somehow passed me by. It might have been in the newspaper or on the radio, an item in my social media feed. It might also not have been reported. A small tragedy that was not big enough news. Not that the details of what occurred really mattered. It was clear enough what the shrine on the bridge represented: that for someone there had been nowhere else than this, no other side of the tracks.

I rested my hands on the railings, on either side of the flowers, and looked out across the railway lines and the construction site, back down to Lost Lane and across to the remnants of a flak tower on a wooded hill. The TV Tower reflected the late afternoon sunlight in the distance and I heard the call of hooded crows and starlings, and the rumble of the orange bin lorries as they crossed the road bridge fifty metres away on their journey to the recycling plant on the other side. Below, in the overgrown triangle of land between the railway lines, there was an edgeland space, surrounded by the city and yet inaccessible to all but the railway workers and the most committed urban explorers. A flash of colour and sudden movement in one of the trees. A screaming call. It was a jay, and I caught the slightest glimpse of the bird before it disappeared once more.

There was a small card attached to the flowers. Without thinking, I leaned down to open it.

Liebe Natascha…

I read those first two words then pulled my hand away, letting the card close once more. It was not a message for me. I tucked the card back into the plastic the flowers were wrapped in, fixed in place by a tightly wound blue rubber band.

I stood there for a little longer, looking out over the city from Natascha's shrine. I stood there with the tracks and the bushes, the birds and the building site, the flowers and the candles. There were some stories of Lost Lane and of the city that I could learn. I could read about them in books or online, in newspaper articles or magazines. There were other stories that were mine, and those told to me by the people who had experienced them. And there were other stories of this city, of these streets and neighbourhoods, these buildings and the spaces in-between, that I had no business knowing at all.

XII

The Haunted Land

It was during my final year in Berlin that Johannes began drinking in the pub. He came on Fridays, to end the working week sitting at the corner of the bar. Johannes went to the pub, he said, to be somewhere different than the places he spent the rest of the week, to be among people different to those he worked with in the tall, glass tower at Potsdamer Platz or at the evening events his bosses expected him to be a part of. He worked as an analyst for a large financial company, the man in the tower whose job it was to predict the movements of the markets and to insulate his employers from the worst impacts of the next crash before it happened. This was all we knew, as Johannes did not like to talk about work. He did not want to be defined by it, by what people expected him to be, when they found out what it was he spent ten to twelve hours a day diligently working on, in his office, twenty storeys above the city streets below.

Instead, Johannes came to the pub to listen to the conversations already taking place along the length of the bar. He would also join in as, although he was not a football fan, for example, he knew enough to talk about the most recent travails of the city's teams. He had a good memory for details, whether the names of grandchildren or wives, upcoming hospital appointments that had been mentioned in passing or the niggling problems of an old car. Johannes did not like to talk about himself, but he enjoyed talking about others, learning about what bothered them, sympathising with a hand on the shoulder and the offer of a drink. In the year or so that I knew him, I never discovered the name of the company he worked at, his relationship status, or even where in the city he lived. He showed no interest in telling anyone these details of his life. To know the Johannes who came once a week to take his place at the end of the bar, it was not important to have these details, and he did not tell me, nor the other drinkers in the pub on those Friday evenings.

There was, however, one part of his life he did not mind speaking about, and that was his village, the place he grew up in, not far from Berlin, where he had lived until he left for university and the place he still called home.

It was a Friday night, early in the year. I was sat at the table by the door, waiting for K. to meet me after she'd finished at the university. Johannes pulled out the chair opposite and sat down, placing a pile of papers on the table between us. I looked from the papers to him, and waited.

'I thought you might be interested,' he said, leaning forward to push them closer to me. They were loose, about five hundred sheets in all, fastened together in the jaws of a large bulldog clip. There was no title page, no title at all, just a top sheet of dense, eleven-point, single-spaced type. I flicked through the first few pages and they were all laid out the same way, all offering no clue as to what I might discover if I began to read.

He had heard I was interested in stories, he explained when I looked up at him. That I had an interest in local history. And this was the story of his village, the history of the place where he'd spent his childhood and adolescence. It had taken many, many months, working mainly on the weekends and the occasional evening in the week. He had visited libraries and ordered rare books online, all part of his attempt to piece together the major events in the story of the village, from the first Germanic settlers until the present day. It was not yet finished, but knowing of my interest in things like that, he'd thought I might like to see it.

Johannes looked down at the table as he spoke, rolling the base of his beer glass against the polished surface. The confident financial analyst, standing at the corner of the bar with his shirtsleeves rolled up and his tie stuffed in his pocket, had been replaced by a nervous author. It was a coming out.

He was not much of a writer, he continued, but he felt this was more important than any work that he did for money. People were too often defined only by how they earned a living, he said, but surely other things were more important? They had to be more important. He did not wait for me to reply, but continued to talk about the book. It was over a thousand pages already and he had just reached the period when his parents had moved there in the 1970s with their toddler son. He was finding this part hard because it was no longer abstract history, but personal. It had become his story.

As he continued to talk, I wondered why he was showing me the manuscript if he was not going to let me read it. This was the only hard copy, and although he had it saved on his computer, he was not yet willing to let it out of his sight. That wasn't why he was showing it to me. The point of showing me, it turned out, was that he wanted to show me the village itself, if I was willing to join him.

A week or so later we met at Alexanderplatz and caught a train east, out through the mix of crumbling brick industrial buildings and GDR-era concrete-slab apartment buildings that lined the railway, until we reached the suburbs of garden allotment colonies and new detached houses that seemed to increase in number every time I took this journey beyond the city limits. Outside it was cold, and although there was no snow on the ground, the gardens and fields beyond the carriage window seemed frozen, the ploughed furrows hard and unyielding.

Johannes pointed out landmarks along the way. A water tower and a stretch of the canal. The parkland where he had spent childhood summers as a member of the Young Pioneers and a sedge of cranes, striding across one of the rutted fields. A new solar farm, visible from space. Once we reached the open countryside, passing yet more fields and patches of woodland, he told me stories of farmers finding the remains of soldiers as they dug. These were stories I had heard from others, but I let him tell me because it seemed important to him that he did.

Outside the window, beneath overcast skies, Brandenburg was dulled. Hooded crows and queues of cars waiting at level crossings. Village houses huddled around a church spire, hoping for protection. A solitary walker, making progress between two fields, following a ditch and a line of poplar trees, skeletal and still.

We disembarked at a station that seemed isolated among the fields and beneath a wide expanse of sky. The village was two kilometres away, down a tree-lined avenue. It was over a thousand years old but not important enough to cause a diversion of the line. They simply built the station where the tracks crossed the road to the next village, Johannes explained, so each day during high school he had to make the walk, once in each direction, to catch the train to the nearest town large enough to have a Gymnasium. He must have made that walk two thousand times, he said, following first a sandy trail between the road and the next field, and later the tarmacked bicycle path, laid in the 1990s. By then, his parents were already thinking of leaving. They had moved there because his mother was a teacher at the village primary school and his father worked at the nearby collective farm. When his father lost that job after reunification, he started selling carpets at one of the large furniture stores that had opened by the motorway junction, fifteen kilometres away. As people left the village, it was announced that the primary school was to close. His parents hung on long enough to get Johannes through his schooling, but once he had gone to university, they went too. Now they lived on the other side of the country, close to the Rhine, approaching retirement.

'The village is dying,' Johannes said, as we approached the first of the houses. It was a residential block, built for the farm workers who were no longer needed. Their apartment had been on the second floor, looking out across a patch of grass that divided the block from the row of garages, each just about large enough for a Trabant. The grass was criss-crossed with muddy tracks, between the garages and the stairwell doors, passing rusted poles that once held up washing lines. Many people had left the village, Johannes continued. Most of the businesses too. He pointed across the road to a residential house, where, above the front window, it was still possible to make out the six letters of a sign long-removed.

KONSUM.

There had not been a grocery store since the mid-1990s, he said. The bakery closed down about ten years after that. The pub shut its doors not long after he had left for university. The village was dying, he repeated, which was why he was so determined to tell its story.

We stopped at the church and walked through the graveyard. His family were not from the village, Johannes said, they had been sent there for work. Half the children in the primary school were kids like him, incomers from elsewhere in the GDR. The other half were from families whose names could be found on the headstones in the churchyard. Children whose families had been in the village for generations. It was not surprising that the incomers left, once the work was gone, but now it was the established families who were also leaving or dying out. All but the most hopeless were gone, he said, to find work and a new house in one of those estates on the edge of the city, those new colonies of McMansions built to the same template but individualised with cosmetic alterations to the roof, a porch, the addition of a carport or a conservatory around the back. The city was doing what it had always done, pulling people towards it, increasing the pressure on those who were already there by adding ever more numbers, drawn by the promise of better times. And all the while, his village died its long, slow death.

I asked him if he had ever thought about coming back. About returning to the village and helping arrest the decline.

Johannes nodded. He had, he said softly, almost under his breath. And one day he would. He had an idea, almost a vision, he continued. An organic farm and accommodation. Seminar rooms and a distillery. Selling nature and schnapps and an escape from what Berlin had become and was becoming, all connected to the land and rooted in the place and its people.

He began to walk on and told me to follow. There was another place he wanted me to see.

It was the very last house, right where the cobbled street that ran through the village turned back to tarmac, snaking away in the distance. The house was set back from the road at the end of a short driveway and was surrounded by a wild, overgrown garden. It had been fenced off, although this barrier was easy to breach, and there had also been an attempt to seal off the interior, but there were gaps, holes in the boards that had been hammered into the frames of windows and doors, and we could hear the wind whistling through the hollowed-out building.

This was the house where the White Lady lived, Johannes said, as we stood at the fence. It had been her house since he was a child, back when the house already stood empty. If the White Lady lived there, no one else could.

It was a statement as definitive as the declarations of the love and scurrilous items of local gossip that had been spray-painted onto the disintegrating walls. In front of us, a path had been flattened through the overgrowth, leading from a hole in the fence to a hole in the wall. There was a scorched fire circle between the brambles, with a pile of charred logs at its heart, alongside discarded beer bottles and cans. I asked Johannes if he wanted to go inside, but he shook his head. He had been in once, he continued, when he was about ten. He never went in there again.

It had been a game, a dare between friends. Whoever went in the furthest, whoever penetrated the house the deepest, whoever got closest to meeting the White Lady: they were the winner. Johannes had made it all the way up to the first floor, passing a hole in the staircase until he reached the upper landing. His friends had long since disappeared. He had won. He could remember standing there and listening. Listening for his friends or other signs from the outside world. But he could hear no conversation from his mates, no sounds of the birds in the trees, the tractors in the fields or the church bells, drifting through the village to where he stood on its very edge. All he could hear was his breathing and the echo it created in the shell of the house. It was dark and it was damp and he was scared.

They all knew the story of the White Lady. That to disturb her was to bring bad luck, to you and your family. There had been the boy in his primary school, a few years older, who had fallen and broken his leg. A family, destroyed by financial ruin. A father, taken away by the Stasi. A woman who suffered a miscarriage. Scarred lives. People had died. That was why they had been told to stay away. Everyone knew it.

But he had gone in anyway.

'I didn't believe the stories,' Johannes said, with a shrug. He had wanted to show his friends, and by extension the whole village, that there was nothing in that house to be frightened of. Not even the rats.

He looked at me.

And then, he continued, as he stood on the landing, he heard something. At first he thought it was a knocking. Someone banging against the wall or a door. A rhythmic beat. One, two, pause. One, two, pause. Then he realised they were footsteps, of someone pacing back and forth in a small room. And then he heard a voice, a woman singing. The voice was gentle, plaintive and beautiful. He could not make out the words, but he could sense a yearning in what she was singing, and that it was a refrain, a chorus repeated, over and over. He could still, all those years later, hear the melody in his memory, the sound of it drifting out from beneath a closed door to where he was standing at the top of the stairs.

The White Lady.

Johannes smiled.

They all knew the story, he said again. The story of the landowner going off to fight in the Thirty Years War. About the landowner's wife having an affair with a travelling minstrel who was passing through. About how the landowner returned from the battlefield to catch them, drowning the minstrel in the village pond before locking his wife away. He returned to the battlefield having left her enough food and water to keep her going until he came back to the house. But he never did. He was killed, fighting the armies of Sweden in the north, and in turn his wife would die too, locked away, cursing her husband and putting a curse on the house.

Johannes gave a dry laugh.

The thing was, he continued, his ten-year-old self had been correct. The story *really* wasn't true. The real White Lady haunted a cursed house in Westphalia, hundreds of kilometres away in the west of Germany. But at some point in the 1960s or 1970s it had become the story of the abandoned house at the edge of their village, a story from the other side of the border. They had invited the White Lady to come and stay with them, like the members of the Baader-Meinhof Gang had been invited to hide out in the GDR, undetected and undisturbed. The White Lady's job was to scare people, and especially children, away from the ruined house on the edge of the village, so that no one would go exploring and no one would get hurt. And so she did, and it worked, until everything changed.

When the Wall came down, Johannes said, the story of the White Lady was returned to Westphalia and they finally learned the story of the house on the edge of the village, and how it came to be a ruin. They learned of the day at the end of the Second World War when the Red Army came, and of the stories that had been advancing ahead of them for weeks. The house had been owned by a German officer, and when it became clear they were going to lose the war, he sent a message to his wife. Get out. Go to the Americans. Go anywhere but don't stay there. But she did not leave. The house had been in her family for generations. It was her home. She was not going to abandon it.

Her husband deserted, travelled west overland to get back to the house, dodging the death commandos as he made his way to the village, where he was distraught to find his wife had ignored his letters. She was still there. Again, he tried to persuade her to leave. Again, she refused. He told her what had been done in the east, what had been done in her name. What was being done in return. But she was not going to leave the house, however much he pleaded.

Johannes gripped the fence with his fingers.

It was a spring morning when the Red Army arrived. Later, when the story was told, some of the details would change, but almost all versions agreed that the husband was wearing his uniform while she was wearing a simple, white peasant dress. There was a bang at the front door. The husband made a final plea. The garden was clear. They could at least try. Gently, and finally, she refused one more time. As the soldiers began to batter at the door, with kicks of heavy boots and swinging rifle butts, the husband climbed the stairs to their bedroom where he put his gun in his mouth. The soldiers found the wife in the living room, sitting calmly in her favourite chair.

Johannes would not tell me what came next, although he was sure I could guess. There was an intensity in his voice, one that told me he *needed* me to know what had happened at that place, that he needed me to understand.

There were different endings to the story, he continued. One was that, when the soldiers had left, the wife had climbed upstairs to where her husband lay and sat down next to him. She took his hand and then lifted a bottle of bleach to her mouth. Drank deep. Burned her insides out.

On the edge of the village, facing the house, there were three beats of silence, and then:

'That is the ending I prefer.'

It was an odd choice of word.

I asked him why they had not told this story in the village. Why they hadn't used the ghosts of the couple to scare the children off. But there were too many reasons, Johannes insisted, and anyway, by then the Russians were their brothers, they were their friends. In any case, it did not matter. Their ghosts did not occupy the house any more than the White Lady did. What he had heard as a ten-year-old was simply his imagination, the creaking of floorboards or sudden gusts of wind. There were no ghosts.

But he did not want to go inside, I said, and Johannes shook his head.

There were no ghosts, he said again, letting his fingers drop from the fence, but the house was still haunted.

'We are still haunted.'

The last time I saw Johannes was a few months after our trip to the village. He was standing in his usual position at the corner of the bar, his beer and a shot of *korn* in place in front of him, talking to the regulars as normal.

He came over to me and pulled up a chair, his face flushed. The book, he said, was finished. He had finally understood what it was supposed to be about. He leaned across the table towards me. It wasn't about the village, he continued, eyes locked onto mine. Not really. It was about Germany. The village represented something bigger. He leaned back, smiling. Didn't I understand? All those stories that he had found, they all represented something deeper. More than just the village. The bodies dug from the fields, the rapes and the suicides, the abandonment and the ruins left behind… they all served a greater purpose. He was insistent. It was only through suffering that a culture could come together to form a true nation. It was only out of the ashes. And that was what was needed now. The village had to die, in order for it to be reborn. The village was Germany.

He stood up and turned to go back to the bar, and then stopped. He rested his fingertips on the table and looked me in the eye. I waited, but there were no more words to be said between us, before he looked away and turned on his heel.

I watched him walk back to the bar, finish his beer and then say his goodbyes. As he passed me again on the way to the door, he leaned forward and rapped his knuckles on the corner of the table, and then he was gone. It was the last time I ever saw him.

And yet: in the weeks and months that followed, I was sure I saw him many, many times, so much so that I almost expected to catch a glimpse of that familiar figure, with its slim face and slightly hunched shoulders. I was convinced it was Johannes I was looking at, even when I saw him from behind. I saw him on a demonstration at the Kaiser-Wilhelm-Memorial Church, where I watched from the counterdemo through the line of police officers and glimpsed him for second between the row of helmets. There was another march, full of German flags and banners, black and gold crosses against a red background. There was a rally on Alexanderplatz, where I was sure I saw him near the front, by the stage, listening intently to the speaker's twisted grasp of history and what it all meant.

I began to see him on television, in front of a theatre on a platform between two poets or on a podium in a market square, occupying the shadows behind the men and women at the microphone. The more I saw him, the more I looked. I did not know his surname, but I searched online, scouring photographs and news footage as the rise of this new movement gathered pace. And there he was. Always in the background, always slightly obscured, but always there.

Johannes was a vision in a huge march at the other end of the country, walking in solidarity with movements in another land. Johannes was standing behind a political candidate, in the media scrum outside a hustings. Johannes was in a YouTube video from a small town in Saxony, sitting on the back of a truck as slogans were shouted through a crackly loudspeaker.

The more I searched, the more convinced I was that I could read Johannes's voice behind anonymous contributions to forums, social media feeds and on comments beneath newspaper articles, hiding behind a range of pseudonyms that represented in words and numbers the nature of the struggle to which he was now committed.

It was getting out of hand, K. said. She could not understand why it mattered, why I cared if it was Johannes or not. What mattered, she said, was that this was happening. Not some person who had once been to the same pub we went to. If I was to use my energy for anything, it should be to try and help win the argument that was now taking place, rather than obsessing over an impossible search for a living ghost.

*

She was right, of course. But one morning I went into the kitchen after she had already gone to the university. On the table she had left a copy of the newspaper, opened on a page that featured an interview with a man who had been photographed outside his comfortable-looking farmhouse in the country. He was a farmer, he told the journalist, and he was committed to the environment. His farm was now completely organic and he was clear that there was a need to break the dependence on oil and other fossil fuels. The way we treated the planet, he said, was a disgrace. But he did not see any contradiction in his environmental politics and his approach to politics elsewhere in society. The extreme left, he continued, seemed to think green issues belonged to them. But they didn't. He loved his country and he loved the land; he understood instinctively that there was a need to protect it, and not despite his nationalism but *because* of it. There was nothing wrong with wanting to protect what you had. Not in nature, nor in culture. And there was nothing wrong in being proud of what you had. In nature and in culture. In what came before.

Beneath the article was a related story. A huge march, crossing a bridge above a wide river in one of Germany's neighbouring lands. Thousands of people beneath a series of ugly, nativist banners. The caption told of hundreds who had travelled there in solidarity from other European countries. One of the faces in the crowd had been circled by K., using a green highlighter pen.

Dein Gespenst geht um in Europa...

K. had scribbled these words in biro down the margin, next to the photograph.

I pulled the newspaper close. I could not be sure if it was

Johannes. In any case, I understood that it did not really matter if it was Johannes, and yet even as I knew this constant search had been pointless, I was still catching glimpses of him, this spectre in the shadows that was now crossing borders. His name appeared on no ballot papers. His work was sold in no bookshops. There were no interviews with him in the newspapers. But he was in all these places nevertheless, and each time I sensed his presence, I wondered again at what he thought he had heard, standing on the landing of the ruined house at the edge of his village. What had the White Lady been singing to him, what was the song that had echoed down through two decades to inform a thousand pages of his book? What was the message and what was it, exactly, that she was calling him to do?

XIII

Archipelago

When Adam came home from work to tell Annika he was leaving, she was down in the workshop, working on an illustration. Isi was upstairs having a nap, and Annika would later remember being annoyed by the noise Adam made as he entered the house, scared that he would wake her. She heard his footsteps as he moved through the rooms above her, heard him stop in the conservatory, to look out across the fields to the river, the same view that was slowly taking shape on the thick paper in front of her. She listened as he turned again, back into the house, and as he walked over to the stairs, footsteps descending to the bottom. She did not look up from her desk as he stood there in doorway, nor as he told her what he had come home early from work to tell her.

There had been no one specific moment that brought them to this point, with Adam standing on one side of the room and Annika sitting at the desk on the other, but she had known it was coming. A slow death. That was how she described the end of her relationship later, once she had left the house behind her to go back to Berlin.

In the workshop, Adam turned and went up to their bedroom to pack a bag. After a minute or two she followed him up the stairs. Now it was her turn to stand in a doorway. As he packed, she was not thinking about him. She did not ask him for reasons. She did not ask him if there was anyone else. If there wasn't now, there would be in the future. The problem, as she saw it then, was not that he might want someone else, it was that he no longer wanted her, and that the feeling had long been mutual. As he packed he tried to talk, but she cut him off. She sensed he wanted to provoke an argument, to try and engineer a moment that would make his leaving justifiable, if only to himself. He wanted to hurt her so that she would be forced to retaliate, so that he could tell himself that the situation was impossible and not really his fault. She refused to return fire. She had the weapons to hurt him, weapons that had been hidden in the forest at the bottom of the hill, but she would not use them.

No blame, she told herself as she watched him pack. No blame on either side. It was the only way they could make it work for Isi. And so she stood in the doorway, the scene unfolding as she had seen it so many times on a TV screen, and she thought about practicalities. Adam had already rented an apartment in the next town over, and in the long run they would sell the house. She would need a better job. They would have to come to arrangements over Isi. And as she stood there, creating the mental checklist of things that needed to be done in the hours, days and weeks that followed, she did not feel any anger or upset. Instead, she told K. later, it was a mix of relief that it could finally all get started, and annoyance at every new item she added to the list.

She returned to the city. There was no alternative plan that she could make work. She met Adam in the town where he now lived and they walked by the lake as she outlined what would happen next. Their house would be sold and the money split between them. It was a ninety-minute drive between Berlin and the town by the lake. She would bring Isi out every second Friday and he would return her to the city on Sunday evening. In the holidays they could split the time more evenly, but for the beginning their daughter needed a stable routine. By this time Adam had lost the desire to provoke, to hurt her, and he agreed to the plan without discussion. At the end, as they said goodbye, there were apologies from both sides, even if Annika did not think there was any point any more. It was over, she thought as she walked away, and it was with dry eyes that she drove back to the house that would soon be nothing but a memory and an unfinished illustration.

In Berlin, she returned not to the city centre that she'd left behind for the house on the ridge, but to the suburbs and her childhood home. If her parents resented the sudden intrusion of their grown-up daughter and four-year-old granddaughter on their peaceful, retired existence, they never let it show. If anything, they treated Annika with a solicitous, careful caution, as if she was sick or bereaved. Annika gave Isi her old room, while she moved into the attic that was usually reserved for guests. She wanted to feel like a temporary visitor. Isi took it all in her stride, starting a new nursery across the street from Annika's old primary school. On the morning walks, the sun still low in the sky, Annika was taken back to her own childhood mornings, decades before. The light and the smell, the sound of the kids in the playground and the parents at the gates. After leaving Isi she walked on to the forest, to be taken to different times and places. She no longer missed the house on the ridge or the view from the conservatory, but she did miss her walks in the woods: the smell of damp leaves and pine cones; the slowly rotting ferns and mushrooms growing on a felled log; the freshness of wild flowers in a clearing; the sweet tang of a blackberry.

After her morning walk, she filled out job applications and helped her parents around the house. In the evenings, after Isi was in bed and the television showed the latest crime drama in the corner of the living room, Annika took refuge in the attic room. There she tentatively began to work on a new map. Before she left Berlin the first time, she believed she'd completed her series of maps. But now she realised there was one more to be done. It was to be a map of Berlin where Berlin did not exist, an imagination of the city without the city. Glacial lakes were to be freed of their stone embankments. Rivers, long forced underground or diverted, would be returned to the surface. Swallowed villages would be allowed to stand alone once more, linked by the old ways and lost lanes that traversed the meadows and marshlands.

Stendhal, her father told her one morning, as she helped him clear out the garage, had never been able to understand why anyone would want to build a town, let alone a city, among all this sand. Annika said that she agreed, and so she was taking it all away.

A month after her return, Annika called K. to see if she wanted to join her for a walk. It was around the time K. had been offered a job in Magdeburg, and was contemplating leaving the city just as her best friend returned to it. They had a lot to talk about, from Annika's situation to whether K. was going to make the journey west. And whether I was going to join her, and what it meant if I didn't.

It was during an election campaign as K. caught the S-Bahn north to the suburban station to meet Annika, and every lamp post in the city was decorated with one, two and sometimes three smiling faces, pitching for votes. The candidates offered competing slogans to offer simple solutions to complex issues. Some were local, like wind farms and housing developments, a proposed abattoir and the new airport. Others were wider, but no less fiercely debated, from the economy to Europe and, more than anything, asylum and immigration.

Outside the station, a huge billboard for a far-right party had been defaced with pink paint.

REFUGEES WELCOME.

The answer was scrawled in black marker pen beneath: FICK DICH.

They walked together through residential streets lined

with posters, before following a cobbled road that ran between a cemetery fence and the sound barrier of the motorway leading out of the city. They were walking towards the river that marked the northern boundary of Berlin, and the trees they could see in the distance were already in Brandenburg, as were the wind farms rotating slowly in the breeze.

As they walked, Annika told K. about how the river had once been navigable, the main communication link between a chain of villages. Now it was a shallow stream lined with tall reeds and, beyond its northern bank, an expanse of grass meadows, sometimes populated by water buffalo. Look left, Annika continued, and you can imagine how this all would have looked before the city spread out so far. She did not tell K. to look right, where, through gaps in the fence, it was possible to see the swing sets and trampolines, gas-fired barbecues and patio furniture of suburban gardens.

Annika's map of the city without the city was not going to be a historical document, she explained. It was not supposed to be an imagination of what once was, but instead a vision of what might have been. She gave an example: where they were standing had once been a crossing point for reindeer on their long migrations thousands of years before, until the climate changed and they moved north to cooler climes. There would be no reindeer on her map, she said, but there would be wolves. A week earlier she had joined a dusk tour through the forest north of Berlin, where the ranger told her about the return of the wolves to the German forests, tens, if not hundreds of years after they had been hunted out of existence. Now, following epic journeys from Russia and Poland, crossing borders both natural and invented, there were over seventeen packs in the countryside around Berlin,

PAUL SCRATON

with more than a hundred and fifty animals in all, and some
had been captured, glassy-eyed in night-vision photographs,
moving inside the Berlin motorway ring. Farmers were
concerned and local hunters were offering their services.
Conservationists tried to spread an alternative view, of the
benefits for biodiversity that the return of the wolves would
bring, but within weeks of the first sighting on German
soil the panic had begun to spread. Images of ripped-
apart calves and other young livestock were disseminated
through the internet. Public meetings were called, along with
demands for action. The government, seeming to side with
the conservationists and the park rangers, offered subsidies
and other financial help to farmers to secure their livestock.
The wolves would find a way, was the pessimistic reply, but
Annika's ranger seemed hopeful nevertheless.

Unless something drastic happened, Annika repeated to
K., the wolves were back for good. Each evening she opened
the window of her parents' attic room as she worked, looking
out across the rooftops to the dark forest beyond, and listened
for their call.

After the tour had finished, Annika had walked on with
the ranger to look at an abandoned holiday camp on the edge
of the nature park. It had been used for school and Young
Pioneer camps in the GDR, and was privatised in the 1990s.
Not long after, it had been closed following an incident
during which two boys had died. They had been fifteen, and
the story that made it into the local newspapers and as far as
Berlin had been that it was some kind of suicide pact. Other
reports suggested an accident with fireworks or a rotten tree
branch. It did not matter what the truth was, the ranger told
Annika. Once the different stories had spread they took root.

They became the truth, even if they were at odds with each other and the reality of what happened that day.

After the incident, the council bought the camp back and made plans to turn it into a residential centre for adults with learning difficulties, before funds were withdrawn and the plans quietly abandoned. The camp was left alone, slowly swallowed by the forest, so that by the time the ranger took Annika there it felt like they were discovering the hidden traces of a lost civilisation. There had been offers to buy the camp in the meantime, although the only one that seemed serious was from a youth organisation with strong neo-Nazi links, whose bid to build an 'education centre' on the site was rejected by the council once those links were exposed by local anti-fascist groups.

Annika and K. continued to walk by the river, their talk of wolves and abandoned holiday camps, lost villages and the sandy ground that was constantly shifting beneath their feet. K. tried to talk about Adam, but Annika was not interested. It was all over now, she said, before returning to her ghosts of the forest and how the sandy soil absorbed all the memories and trauma of what had happened above it. Most of all, she was exercised by what people had done, both to the landscape and to each other, and how everything that happened somehow remained there, whether she included it in her maps or not, from the malignant impact of the city on its surroundings to the deep, cultural memory of events hundreds of years past. She spoke of the Thirty Years War and the rise in superstition and belief in witchcraft. It was not only the poor who believed in forces they could not see, but also the educated and the aristocracy. Princes saw spectres threatening their fortunes and theologians blamed ghosts for deaths in the family. Wealthy landowners arranged for the exorcism of cursed wives and all the while people tried to forget their situation by drowning themselves in beer and wine. Some things, she said with a smile, remained the same.

On the path by the river, they looked across a fence to where an oversized German flag was flying in a garden.

'Do you remember there being flags when we were kids?' K. asked.

The two friends agreed that they could not.

They lost the river into the bog from which it came, and followed the path as it crossed a meadow towards a village, built on a small rise overlooking the tower blocks of a housing estate that had been built on the very edge of the city. They came to a bench where they sat with a flask of coffee and a packet of biscuits that Annika produced from her bag.

'Every street in Berlin is lower than we are now,' she said, as they passed the cup of coffee back and forth between them. There was a projection she had seen online, she continued, as they looked back towards the city. It was a map of Germany in the year 2100 and the result of catastrophic climate change. It looked, she said, as if a bite had been taken out of the country. The whole of the north was under water. Hamburg, Stralsund, Rostock and Berlin were all marked on the map as 'sunken cities'. The coastline of Germany's mainland now followed a chain of towns along what had once been the Via Regia, a medieval trading route that passed through Thuringia. Deep, inland cities like Erfurt, Weimar and Eisenach were now ports, offering ferry connections to Sweden and Norway, as well as to what had become known as the Northern Islands, a scattered archipelago of places that had not quite succumbed to the rising waves.

'*And the rain fell,*' Annika said, '*and the floods came, and the winds blew and beat against that house, and it fell, and great was the fall of it.*'

The largest town close to Berlin that would survive the flood, she continued, was Bad Freienwalde. This spa town, fifty kilometres north of the city, would become the main settlement on one of the Northern Islands. It was this information, and the projection that Annika had discovered online, that had led her to a new plan. Once the house she had shared with Adam was sold, she would use her share to start again in Bad Freienwalde. It was a long-term plan, and not so much for her, or even Isi, but perhaps for Isi's children.

You can't take it with you, she said, but you can leave it behind.

They sat on the bench for hours, until there was no coffee left and the biscuit packet was empty. Annika sketched out for K. her further plans for Bad Freienwalde. She wanted to get a job with the National Parks or the forestry service, perhaps leading guided tours into the forest. She wanted to work outdoors, under open skies and the canopies of trees, and she wanted to see the return of the wolves to Brandenburg with her own eyes.

When K. returned that evening, she told me the story of the walk and the things they had spoken about, but I knew there were parts of the story she left out. There was no mention of Magdeburg and the job offer, about whether she would be leaving Berlin and whether she would be leaving alone. If she had spoken to Annika about it, she did not want to speak about it to me, because it was a conversation neither of us was ready for. She did not tell me what she had told Annika and what Annika had said in return, and I did not ask. We were not there yet. It still felt like a journey that was moving to a conclusion, and we simply had to wait for the destination to come into view.

Undressed, she climbed into bed next to me. With her tablet she switched on the evening news via a television live stream. The election campaign was dominating, as the faces that looked down on us from every lamp post were now animated, making speeches or moving with purpose along the campaign trail. With every utterance you could sense fear. It was written in their eyes. Had something changed, even while they had been talking? The campaign trail was a road that supposedly travelled in a straightforward direction, but they knew that wasn't the case. Underneath their feet, the trail was shifting. It was always shifting.

After a minute or two K. gave up, switched off the tablet, and rolled over onto her side. I listened as her breathing changed, becoming deeper and more regular. It would be a while before I was ready to sleep. Instead, I pictured the two friends, looking down on the city as they imagined everything they could see sunken beneath the Baltic waves. Meadows and marshes, apartment blocks and detached houses, the places they had lived and gone to school, worked and loved, argued and fucked. The sun was falling in the sky as they sat there, poised and waiting; one decided, the other trying to make a decision. The latter couldn't get there because it was not a decision she could make alone, and the words were not there yet.

Swallows swooped and dived in the fading light, the mosquitoes of the marsh providing an evening feast. The friends talked, back and forth, and then there was silence for a moment, before Annika began to speak once more.

'*After the flood there was again a beginning,*' she said, resting her head on her friend's shoulder as the sun met the horizon.

XIV

Feierabend Bier

For Hobrecht, the idea of walking the city began with a trip to the Botanical Gardens, back in the early weeks after he had been made redundant, when he was still working out how best to fill his days. He caught the S-Bahn south and emerged onto the street outside the Botanischer Garten station where, he would later admit, he got lost. Back and forth he wandered through a neighbourhood that, as he walked, he realised he had never been to before despite more than fifty years as a Berliner. He wandered the tidy streets named for flowers and plants, stopped to gaze at the window displays of antique dealers and old-fashioned stationers, read the memorial plaques on the sides of buildings and explored the different types of properties on offer at a local estate agents. By the time he found the entrance to the Botanical Gardens, he realised he had lost interest in going inside, so he continued to walk, zigzagging through the neighbourhood as he got ever closer to the large, black tower block that had become his accidental target. Once there, he walked on, following a shopping street lined with the same brand names he could find in the mall across the street from where he lived, before ducking down side streets where he noticed the difference in architectural styles between this neighbourhood and his own on the other side of the city. He stopped for coffee on the second floor of a shopping centre that looked out across the street at an abandoned modernist observation tower, and felt a shiver of recognition that led to a dim memory of a visit, perhaps with his parents, when there was still a restaurant offering views of a six-lane motorway and the city skyline beyond. By this point he had been walking for a couple of hours, and that was the first place in all that time that he recognised, that he was conscious of having been to before.

As the walks continued, over the following weeks and months, he realised that he was moving between the different places of his memory, filling in the blank spaces between them as he went. The more he walked, the more he realised how little he knew of the city of his birth, and how, with each step along the pavement, he was bringing his own personal and fragmented city together for the very first time.

Hobrecht started to walk because he had lost his job, because he was officially unemployed but there was only so much time he could spend at the library filling in job applications or sitting in that stuffy office at the Agentur für Arbeit, where the friendly caseworker explained to him that he needed to be patient, and that it would not be easy for a man in his fifties to find an equivalent job to the one that had let him go in the name of company restructuring. But beyond a simple need to fill the hours of the day that had become a quest to better understand his home town, Hobrecht walked because he needed to be out of the house. And he needed to be out of the house because he had never told his wife about losing his job. Early on he made the calculations, working out that his redundancy money and unemployment benefits would bridge the gap until he found a new job. With each day that passed and with each continuation of the charade that was played out each morning and evening in their apartment in Reinickendorf, the harder it became to tell her truth. Perhaps it was this that led him to the pub a few evenings a week, which was where I met him, to steel himself for the next in the increasingly long line of small lies that could all be traced back to the first, big one. Not that Hobrecht called them lies. He preferred to describe them as 'gentle untruths', designed to protect. There were many, including how he introduced himself to us on one of those early evenings in the pub. We later learned that his real name was something different, although I continued to call him Hobrecht even after that particular gentle untruth had been revealed.

Once he started his walks, Hobrecht split his time in the local library between filling out the next job application and planning the next of his excursions through the city. He started in the centre of town, following the schoolbook story of the city past the landmarks that defined the main periods of the city's history. Palaces and churches, museums and memorials. He explored the centre of Berlin for traces of the

Kaiser, of Hitler and the German Democratic Republic, the remnants of regimes in this city where theories were tested on the ground and where they all seemed destined to fail while leaving their mark in the buildings and the memories of the people. What struck Hobrecht on those early walks, along streets and across squares, was how much work was still going on to reshape the city. Everywhere he went he came across yet more cranes and diggers, and more pink pipes emerging from the ground where they pumped out the water that threatened to sink the foundations of buildings not yet built, part of the never-ending battle to hold back the return of the Berlin swamp.

Hobrecht walked to the sound of drills and jackhammers as he crossed the strange expanse of emptiness between the Reichstag and the new train station, where gaps created by war and division were still to be filled as part of yet another attempt to tilt the axis of the city and recentre Berlin once more. From the dust and the noise of the construction sites he fled along a canal embankment, past the military hospital and the cemetery where fragments of the Berlin Wall still stood. There was a watchtower there, hemmed in by apartments, and a row of brand new townhouses outside which children played on a perfect stretch of tarmac across the water from a giant wasteland, long home to nothing but crows picking over the rubble and the occasional travelling circus, but which had now been earmarked as the next major place of residential and commercial development.

He could remember the other construction waves in the city, from his childhood in the 1960s and through the decades that followed. After the Wall came down he had walked across the no man's land of Potsdamer Platz, once the neon-lit epicentre of *Weltstadt*-Berlin in the 1920s, transformed by Anglo-American bombs and the sector boundary that ran right through it into an abandoned rabbit run. After the Wall it became a huge sandbox, in preparation for the global architectural elite to come and unleash their vision on the city and to mark in steel, glass and concrete the next new era. Hobrecht's walk from the main station took him along the fringes of the Tiergarten park, past the Memorial to the Murdered Jews of Europe and the Canadian Embassy to Potsdamer Platz, where he tried to work out where he had stood in the early 1990s, gazing across the empty space towards East Berlin through a hole that had been punched in the Wall.

It was history that shaped many of Hobrecht's walks, offering a theme to guide him from one place to another. He searched for traces of the old villages and towns that made up Berlin before it was Berlin, looking for visual links back in time to when each stood alone, with its own sense of community and identity, when the travelling singers who moved from one to the other rewrote their ballads in each to suit local tastes. He took a walk following the route of the old Customs Wall that had encircled the city until the middle of the nineteenth century. Barely anything remained of this alternative Berlin wall, but he could trace its route by going gate to gate – Oranienburger Tor, Hallesches Tor, Frankfurter Tor – which still gave their names to U-Bahn stations and other places on his city map, long after all but the most famous had been destroyed.

As time went on, he invented reasons or themes upon which to base his walks. One led him between the different IKEA stores in the city, inspired by a story he had read from the Thirty Years War, when the occupying Swedish armies in Berlin forced confessions from subjects by making them drink a mix of piss and shit. This was known as *Schwedentrunk* – the Swedish drink. As Hobrecht walked from one big box of blue and yellow to the next, he reflected that the modern invasion was much more benign, based as it was on beds and bookcases and plenty of meatballs.

One theme led to another. From Swedish Berlin he went on to explore the sewage fields of the Industrial Revolution, wandering the old irrigation systems created to manage the human waste of the rapidly growing metropolis, now transformed into nature parks or semi-wild spaces. In truth, it was these in-between spaces that Hobrecht liked the best, places that had become the preserve of no one but the dog walkers, the joggers and the lonely explorers. Hobrecht saw them all as his co-conspirators, forging their desire paths across scrappy patches of otherwise forgotten grassland, or along the edges of forbidden zones, creating tracks through the undergrowth alongside high, wire fences, topped with spikes.

At a computer terminal in the library, Hobrecht tracked his walks on a map after he had completed each one, marking out his route in red. Slowly he was filling in the city, and as time passed, he could see more clearly the gaps, the parts of the city he had not yet reached. As the first year of his unemployment progressed, he became ever more determined to fill them in, to cover the whole city with his thin red lines. It was around this time that he told me what it was he was up to. It was both a form of confession and a desire to tell someone about the ever-expanding network of lines on his map. He wanted to show me, because it was beginning to feel, in Hobrecht's mind, like an achievement. He began to tell me about his walks, about the slow discovery of his city and, of course, the gentle untruth that had started it all.

That day he had been to Gropiusstadt, right on the very southern edge of Berlin, where the balconies of the apartment blocks looked out beyond the city limits and into Brandenburg. He had fallen into conversation with the woman who owned the florist shop outside the U-Bahn station and within sight of what Hobrecht had read was Germany's tallest residential building. It was true, the florist told him. She knew, she said, because she lived there, right on the top floor. She asked him if he wanted to see, and although Hobrecht demurred, she insisted. She was due a break anyway. And so he followed her on the short walk across the concourse and through the trees, past the playground that stood at the foot of the tower, and into an elevator that lifted them up, high above the rest of the neighbourhood.

From her balcony they could see much of Gropiusstadt laid out around them and then, to the south, it simply stopped. Tower blocks on one side of the street, farmed fields on the other. The reason for the abrupt shift from urban to rural was the Berlin Wall, which had once divided Gropiusstadt from the surrounding countryside, and although the watchtowers and concrete slabs were long gone, the shift from one to the other remained as stark as it had ever been. The florist had been in her teens when the Wall came down, and she could remember Gropiusstadt back then, and the special checkpoint that allowed West Berlin's refuse lorries to access a rubbish tip in the Brandenburg fields. It was one way, she said, for the East Germans to make some hard currency. Now they were turning that into a park as well. Rubbish tips and sewage fields, all transformed by grass and gravel pathways.

What Hobrecht liked about his walks, he told me, was that they allowed him to understand both the layout of the city, the geography and topography, but also its rhythms. He had started to get a sense of its routines and structures, of when were the best times to stop for lunch or which U-Bahn stations would be at their busiest when he was travelling to and from his walks. He knew which benches by the Spree would be nicely in the shade on a summer lunchtime and where to go to catch the murmuration of starlings at dusk. He could tell which streets were truly residential, and which had been given over almost entirely to short-term holiday lets and how busy they would be, depending on the day of the week or the time of year.

He could see, now, how to trace the changes in the city just by looking. Not because the clues hadn't been there before, but because he'd never lifted his eyes in the first place.

The last time I saw Hobrecht was on the final night in Franz's pub. A few months before, Franz had received a letter from the owners of the building. His contract was about to expire, and although they were happy to offer him a new one, they also wanted to increase the rent. It was too much, Franz said, to justify the work. What had begun as a sociable way to top-up his policeman's pension was about to turn into a struggle.

Franz was not bitter, he simply saw it as a sign that it was time to move on, and wrote back to politely decline the offer and to make a date for the handover of the keys. A few days before he would host the last night in the pub, working the bar himself: a chance for everyone to say goodbye.

As I arrived that evening I realised how few of my fellow drinkers I knew. There was Markus, in the corner, who had come into town from his cabin in the countryside to make this final farewell. Charlotte would arrive later, still trying to decide on her plans now that she had finished her doctorate. But most of those I had spent long evenings with in that unassuming pub on the corner of a nondescript street had already moved on. That night, those of us who were there continued to drink as if we did not want the final evening to end. At around three, Franz locked the doors and those who remained sat at the long table beneath the window, and whoever wanted another drink simply helped themselves. Franz was, he said, already three hours into his retirement.

I left the pub as the city was beginning to wake, the sun bright in my eyes as I started the walk home. As I walked, it was not those who had been there during Franz's long last night that occupied my thoughts, but those who had been absent. Tomas and Boris. Otto and Konrad. Annika. Johannes. This was the problem with farewells. It made you think of all the things you had lost.

As I stood among the smokers congregating on the pavement in the evening sunshine, a few hours earlier, I had pulled out my phone and pictured K., sitting on the sofa of her apartment in Magdeburg, watching one of her crime shows as my message was delivered. Her reply came within a couple of beats. She wished she could be there with us too.

✳

Earlier that day, Hobrecht had been for a walk around the Botanical Gardens, only this time he'd been inside. The flowers were beautiful at this time of year, he said, as we stood at the bar together, but then again, he had nothing to compare them with. He called Franz over to order me a drink.

'I think I've made a decision,' he said, rubbing the side of his face with his hand. 'I think it is time that I told her.'

It was nearly a year since that first walk, he continued, and the money was about to dry up. If he did not find a job soon, he would have to apply for a different type of benefits. He could maintain the charade no longer. And there seemed little prospect of a job. His caseworker was growing increasingly concerned. So he would have to come clean.

I tried to imagine the moment. The outpouring of truth. The sense of betrayal. Could a relationship survive such a revelation? What would emerge from that wreckage? But if Hobrecht was concerned about what he was about to do, it wasn't showing. He seemed tranquil as we stood at the bar, watching Franz slowly pour the beers.

I asked him if this meant he had finished walking, and he agreed.

'Is the map finished?'

He looked at me with an indulgent smile.

'No,' he said. 'That would be impossible. It's like painting the bridge in Scotland. By the time you've finished, you'd have to start again. No, it's not finished. But it's enough.'

The beers arrived and we touched glasses. A toast to the end of the road.

✳

That evening in the pub, I thought about Hobrecht's walks and how little I knew of the city after all the years of living there. I was paid to tell people the stories of Berlin, but I could only ever know a tiny fraction. Even Hobrecht, with his map covered in red, could only speak of part of the story. Wasn't that true? He looked thoughtful when I asked him.

'Have you ever sat at the window on a flight into Berlin?' he asked, after a moment's pause. It never failed to make him marvel, he continued, at the location of the city. Why had they built it there? Viewed from above, its existence made no sense. There was no coastline, no major river. It was part of no ancient trade routes of any consequence. From above, Hobrecht said, when you looked down at this place surrounded by lakes and forests, where the trees seemed to reach into the very city itself as if to remind everyone that they could retake this occupied ground at any moment, it was clear that this was somewhere that had simply been willed into existence. It was here because someone had wanted it to be. Nothing more, nothing less.

But there was something else that he felt from that window seat, as the plane approached Tegel or Schönefeld. As he looked down on the lakes and the forests of Brandenburg, the paper mills and open-cast mines scraped out of the sandy soil, and as the city grew closer, with its tenement blocks and housing estates, streets and squares, parks and playgrounds, he realised that he could see more than just the view from above. From his window seat he could picture what was down there on the ground because of his many walks. Certain landmarks triggered memories. The cooling tower or the power station. The hospital grounds or a stretch of canal, narrow between the weeping willows. Coming in to land, he had that sense of recognition that came at the end of a long road trip, as you drove along the first street in your neighbourhood that was part of your normal, daily routine. When you passed by the church or the local supermarket where you shopped, your child's school or the tram stop where you waited each morning on the way to work. These were the places that made you understand that the journey was now over. That even before you came to a stop, you were already home. For Hobrecht, because of his walks, because of what he saw when he looked down from above as the plane came in to land, this feeling was now embedded in every corner of Berlin.

'You can't know it all,' he said. 'But you know something. At that's what makes it feel like home. That's what makes you feel you belong. And it is open to anyone, whether you were born here or if you've only just arrived. I was born in this city over fifty years ago. It is only now that I feel this… this feeling of being rooted. It is not about birth. You don't inherit it. You choose to be part of it. By walking and talking, by listening and learning the stories of others. That's what makes you belong.'

He finished his drink and offered me his hand. It was time to go home and talk to his wife.

After Hobrecht had left the pub I stood alone at the bar, imagining what it was he saw when he looked down from the window seat as the plane came in to land. The city, fanning out around the TV Tower. The apartment buildings and the boulevards, the scraps of green and the ribbons of grey. I thought of the invisible places in the city and beyond, hidden by walls or the dense canopy of the trees. The abandoned house on the edge of a slowly dying village. A holiday camp, overgrown and crumbling. Bodies in the woods, buried in shallow graves. Wild boar and wolves, and women in white dresses. And I thought of the stories I didn't know. Those of my neighbours and those who lived in a Zehlendorf villa or a Spandau apartment block. The fourth-generation Turkish-German family across the courtyard or the woman in my local supermarket whose name suggested she was descended from Huguenots. The residents of the white Tempohomes, hidden away behind a rubble mountain, between the clay courts of the tennis club and the neat lawns of a garden colony.

The view from the window seat would encompass them all, and there was only so much you could know. And the view from the window seat, it came to me as I asked Franz for another drink, would be the same whether the plane was descending to its destination or climbing up towards the clouds. It would be the same on arrival as it was on departure, as it left the city behind, the view from above part of a final farewell.

Acknowledgements

Thanks once again to Gary, Kit, Sanya and Influx Press for all their support, and to Dan, Austin and Vince for their work on the book.

Thanks to all my family, whether they speak English, German or something in between. Many of the places in this book are places we have explored together.

Thanks to Jessica and Charlotte for getting me to think about haunted lands and the stories I might want to tell.

Thanks to Tom and Jas, Eymelt and Óli, Marcel and Anne, for their support and inspiration.

Thanks to everyone who has helped me explore and get to know Berlin over the past sixteen years and especially the Grey Sky Appreciation Society for walking with me.

I would also like to use the chance to thank all the different writers whose books on Berlin inspired me to discover more of the stories of this city I have come to call home. Those I would particularly like to acknowledge here are all well worth reading for anyone interested in learning more about the history and culture of Berlin: David Clay Large (*Berlin*, Basic Books), Brian Ladd (*The Ghosts of Berlin*, University of Chicago Press), Giles MacDonogh (*Berlin*, St Martin's Press), Mary Fulbrook (*The People's State*, Yale University Press), Antony Beevor (*Berlin: The Downfall 1945*, Penguin), Rory MacLean (*Berlin: Imagine a City*, Orion), Frederick Taylor (*The Berlin Wall*, Bloomsbury), Timothy Garton Ash (*The File*, Atlantic Books) and Neil MacGregor (*Germany: Memories of a Nation*, Penguin).

Finally, and most of all, thanks to my two Berliners. Katrin and Lotte, this is for you.

About the Author

Paul Scraton is a writer and editor based in Berlin. Born in Lancashire, he moved to the German capital in 2001 where he has lived ever since. He is the editor-in-chief of *Elsewhere: A Journal of Place* and the author of *Ghosts on the Shore: Travels Along Germany's Baltic Coast* (Influx Press, 2017). His essays on place and memory have been published as the pocket book *The Idea of a River: Walking out of Berlin* by Readux Books in March 2015, and in *Mauerweg: Stories from the Berlin Wall Trail*, published by Slow Travel Berlin in 2014 to mark the 25th anniversary of the fall of the Berlin Wall. Among other publications, you can find more of Paul's writing on place on *Caught by the River* and in *hidden europe* magazine.

T: @underagreysky W: underagreysky.com

INFLUX
PRESS

Influx Press is an independent publisher based in London, committed to publishing innovative and challenging fiction, poetry and creative non-fiction from across the UK and beyond. Formed in 2012, we have published titles ranging from award-nominated fiction debuts and site-specific anthologies to squatting memoirs and radical poetry.

www.influxpress.com
www.patreon.com/InfluxPress
@Influxpress

GHOSTS ON THE SHORE:
TRAVELS ALONG GERMANY'S BALTIC COAST
Paul Scraton

'A powerful story of human tragedy and its inheritances, of "the hubris of territorial ambition" – less a story of a landscape than of a shifting culture and people.'
— *Times Literary Supplement*

'Deeply immersive and richly braided.'
— Julian Hoffman, author of *The Small Heart of Things*

'Paul Scraton should be encouraged to go on more long walks.'
— *Hidden Europe*

Inspired by his wife's collection of family photographs from the 1930s and her memories of growing up on the Baltic coast in the GDR, Paul Scraton set out to travel from Lübeck to the Polish border on the island of Usedom, an area central to the mythology of a nation and bearing the heavy legacy of trauma.

Exploring a world of socialist summer camps, Hanseatic trading towns long past their heyday and former fishing villages surrendered to tourism, Ghosts on the Shore unearths the stories, folklore and contradictions of the coast, where politics, history and personal memory merge to create a nuanced portrait of place.

ISBN: 9781910312100

THE STONE TIDE:
ADVENTURES AT THE END OF THE WORLD
Gareth E. Rees

'Simultaneously quotidian and grotesque, The Stone Tide is the funniest, most readable, most intelligently self-searching book I've read in years.'
— M John Harrison, author of *Light*

'The problems started the day we moved to Hastings...'

When Gareth E. Rees moves to a dilapidated Victorian house in Hastings he begins to piece together an occult puzzle connecting Aleister Crowley, John Logie Baird and the Piltdown Man hoaxer. As freak storms and tidal surges ravage the coast, Rees is beset by memories of his best friend's tragic death in St Andrews twenty years earlier. Convinced that apocalypse approaches and his past is out to get him, Rees embarks on a journey away from his family, deep into history and to the very edge of the imagination. Tormented by possessed seagulls, mutant eels and unresolved guilt, how much of reality can he trust?

The Stone Tide is a novel about grief, loss, history and the imagination. It is about how people make the place and the place makes the person. Above all it is about the stories we tell to make sense of the world.

ISBN: 9781910312070

HOW THE LIGHT GETS IN
Clare Fisher

'Cements her position as an innovative literary talent.'
— *New Statesman*

'Fisher's tales are funny and moving, and you'll treasure them all.'
— *Stylist*

'If fiction was a language, Clare Fisher would be one of its native speakers: a writer whose whole response to the world is brilliantly story-shaped.'
— Francis Spufford, author of *Golden Hill*

How The Light Gets In is the first collection from award winning short story writer and novelist, Clare Fisher. A book of very short stories that explores the spaces between light and dark and how we find our way from one to the other.

From buffering Skype chats and the truth about beards, to fried chicken shops and the things smartphones make you less likely to do when alone in a public place, Fisher paints a complex, funny and moving portrait of contemporary British life.

ISBN: 9781910312124

ATTRIB. AND OTHER STORIES
Eley Williams

WINNER OF THE JAMES TAIT BLACK PRIZE 2018

WINNER OF THE REPUBLIC OF CONSCIOUSNESS PRIZE 2018

'She is a writer for whom one struggles to find comparison, because she has arrived in a class of her own.'
— Sarah Perry, author of *Melmoth*

'It's just the real inexplicable gorgeous brilliant thing this book. I love it in a way I usually reserve for people.'
— Max Porter, author of *Lanny*

Attrib. and Other Stories celebrates the tricksiness of language just as it confronts its limits. Correspondingly, the stories are littered with the physical ephemera of language: dictionaries, dog-eared pages, bookmarks and old coffee stains on older books. This is writing that centres on the weird, tender intricacies of the everyday where characters vie to 'own' their words, tell tall tales and attempt to define their worlds.

With affectionate, irreverent and playful prose, the inability to communicate exactly what we mean dominates this bold debut collection from one of Britain's most original new writers.

ISBN: 9781910312162

BINDLESTIFF

Wayne Holloway

'A devastating vision of what America is becoming, wrapped up in a compelling and compassionate fable of what it is today.'
— Krishnan Guru-Murthy

'Mixes the drug-fuelled escapades of Hunter S. Thomson with the subversive flair of Colson Whitehead.'
— *Buzz*

2036. In a ramshackle, backwater United States, Marine Corp vet Frank Dubois journeys from L.A. to Detroit, seeking redemption for a life lived off the rails, in a country derailed from its own manifest destiny.

In present day Hollywood, a wannabe British film director hustles to get his movie 'Bindlestiff' off the ground starring 'Frank', a black Charlie Chaplin figure cast adrift in post-federal America.

Weaving together prose and screenplay *Bindlestiff* explores the power and responsibility of storytelling, revealing what lies behind the voices we read and the characters we see on screen. We open with a simple image of a man mending a hole in his shoe using a cut off piece of rubber and a tube of glue. From there the story explodes into a broiling satire on race, identity, family, friendship, war, peace, sex, drugs but precious little rock and roll.

ISBN: 9781910312292

MOTHLIGHT
Adam Scovell

'One of the most interesting and original young British writers
about landscape, culture and people that I know; consistently
adventurous in his explorations of place as a novelist, essayist,
critic and film-maker.'
— Robert Macfarlane

'Adam Scovell is an archaeologist of the imagination, forever
unearthing stories like treasure from the soil, raising ghosts,
finding links and shining a flickering light into England's
hidden corners.'
— Benjamin Myers, author of *The Gallows Pole*

Phyllis Ewans, a prominent researcher in Lepidoptera and a
keen walker, has died of old age. Thomas, a much younger
fellow researcher of moths first met Phyllis when he was a
child. He became her carer and companion, having rekindled
her acquaintance in later life.

Increasingly possessed by thoughts that he somehow
actually is Phyllis Ewans, and unable to rid himself of the feeling
that she is haunting him, Thomas must discover her secrets
through her many possessions and photographs, before he is
lost permanently in a labyrinth of memories long past.

Steeped in dusty melancholy and analogue shadows,
Mothlight is an uncanny story of grief, memory and the price
of obsession.

ISBN: 9781910312377

SIGNAL FAILURE:
LONDON TO BIRMINGHAM, HS2 ON FOOT
Tom Jeffreys

'Through it all, Jeffreys's writing is intelligent, engaging and engaged, and deeply and disarmingly human.'
— *New Statesman*

'Tom Jeffreys is a worthy member of J.B.Priestley's good companions, and *Signal Failure* an engaging and affectionate update on that earlier writer s seminal English Journey.'
— Ken Worpole, author of *The New English Landscape*

One November morning, Tom Jeffreys set off from Euston Station with a gnarled old walking stick in his hand and an overloaded rucksack. His aim was to walk the 119 miles from London to Birmingham along the proposed route of HS2. Needless to say, he failed.

Over the course of ten days of walking, Jeffreys meets conservationists and museum directors, fiery farmers and suicidal retirees. From a rapidly changing London, through interminable suburbia, and out into the English countryside, Jeffreys goes wild camping in Perivale, flees murderous horses in Oxfordshire, and gets lost in a landfill site in Buckinghamshire. *Signal Failure* weaves together poetry and politics, history, philosophy and personal observation to form an extended exploration of people and place, nature, society, and the future.

ISBN: 9781910312148

MARSHLAND:
DREAMS AND NIGHTMARES ON THE EDGE OF LONDON
Gareth E. Rees

'Whatever it is, New Weird, Cryptozoology, Psychogeography or Deep Map, *Marshland* is simply essential reading.'
— *Caught by the River*

'*Marshland* is essential reading – a psychedelic trip into London's secret wilderness.'
— John Rogers, author of *This Other London*

'I had become a bit part in the dengue-fevered fantasy of a sick city.'

Cocker spaniel by his side, Gareth E. Rees wanders the marshes of Hackney, Leyton and Walthamstow, avoiding his family and the pressures of life. He discovers a lost world of Victorian filter plants, ancient grazing lands, dead toy factories and tidal rivers on the edgelands of a rapidly changing city. Ghosts are his friends.

As strange tales of bears, crocodiles, magic narrowboats and apocalyptic tribes begin to manifest themselves, Rees embarks on a psychedelic journey across time and into the dark heart of London.

Marshland is a deep map of the east London marshes, a blend of local history, folklore and weird fiction, where nothing is quite as it seems.

ISBN: 9780957169395

Influx Press lifetime supporters

Barbara Richards
Bob West